CASTHEN GAIN

A NOVELLA OF THE GRAVEN

ESSA HANSEN

Acquiring Editor: Adrian Collins
Copy Editor: Ed Crocker
Cover Artist: Carlos Diaz
Cover Design and Interior Layout: Pen Astridge

Hardcover ISBN: 978-1-923459-00-7
Paperback ISBN: 978-1-923459-01-4
Ebook ISBN: 978-0-6486635-6-0
Worldwide Rights.

Published by Grimdark Magazine
Cannon Hill, QLD, 4170
www.grimdarkmagazine.com

For Vaith, who time could not completely bury.

1

ROUGH CROWD

Head swaddled in sensory deprivation veils, body in aggressive multi-species restraints, and crammed in a prisoner dropship with... he could smell at least twelve others despite the veil... this wasn't the worst outcome Sentace Ketch had imagined after being taken captive. He hadn't been tortured or murdered yet, and he hadn't found Evi dead before he could fake her death himself.

Upside: he was finally free of his attending "team" whose imbecility had gotten him captured in the first place, and whose oversight had meant he'd have to assassinate Evi for real. Everything would be easier now, alone, if he survived whatever this was.

The ship hit atmosphere. A blast of resistance gripped the vessel. Wailing tones transferred to Sentace's skull through the restraints, barely dulled by the material of the veils. The rumbling juddered his teeth. His brain hit a panic switch: stomach acid rose to the base of his throat, urgently swallowed before it reached his tongue. Planetary arrivals and departures were yet another new experience for him, coming from a backwater homeworld galaxies away. This re-entry wasn't helped by the fact that the dropship felt extremely budget, a cacophony of rattles, buzzes, and engine strain.

Eventually the descent evened out and velocity waned. Sentace's stomach continued to argue. He summoned calm. Endure, be patient. His kitchen had taught him patience: dough rising, stock simmering, meat marinating, egg whites stiffening. A rhythm of action and waiting.

In a swift motion, everyone's sensory veils were husked off.

The prisoners exploded into reactions as intense as the restraints allowed. Sentace flinched, his extra-keen human senses assaulted by growling and argument and groaning steel and stomps and one creature wailing what was either despair or a war cry. Sentace was familiar with many species—dining patrons, tourists—but the immense diversity in the multiverse beyond his little planet had shown him just how small his life experience truly was.

Some prisoners recognized one another. A gigantic chketin erupted in uncontrollable laughter while barking out the words, "In here with the scum and scraps, eh, Molinar!"

The chketin's spittle crossed the way to an elderly woman with dark, leathery skin and classical beauty, whose expression remained completely unbothered. Golden jewelry wound her head and neck, and metallic paint sketched expensive flowers around her eyes. High-ranking; someone for whom this capture was a humiliation. Perhaps, in her case, being marked as an expendable utility was the worst possible punishment. All damned, what had Sentace been hurtled into?

Another creature said through a voice box, "Oi, I know you, scrap! Second time caught, eh!" The untranslated language was chemical, wafting into Sentace's nostrils in a cadence of sour prickles and rot-sweet slides.

Face scrunching, he held his breath and tuned out his fellows' overreactions. There were fourteen others, a mix of xenids—he'd nearly guessed right. Hybrid organic-mechanical restraints served as passenger cradles, holding everyone upright and immobile on both ship walls. None looked to have been disarmed or disrobed, though the restraints made attack impossible. Sentace noted that his bandolier of seasonings still looped his chest, and he hoped his chef's vari-knife remained strapped on his thigh.

He tried to catalogue all fourteen potential allies or opponents. A human girl hid behind a curtain of dull blonde hair, her body dewy with drug-sweat, and a glaze of trauma over her fish-pale eyes. The chketin: a species that always looked like charred meat to Sentace, with rough, hairless skin wrapping a thick, muscular frame. Next to a human man with two augmented legs and one hundred percent criminal vibes was a fully mechanical, semi-humanoid exoskeleton with no original body inside. The brain-pan contained a small, squid-like organism that must have been controlling the frame. Beside them was a bipedal xenid, a confusing mass of bone and cartilage.

All in all, the majority of the crowd were humans, though Sentace had come to understand that "human" was an almost uselessly broad term encapsulating such variety it was pointless to attempt to group them properly. Sentace bet his Trowan phenotype was distinct enough to recognize—maybe even by his eyes alone—given how isolated and xenophobic his culture was.

As the most worldly Trowan citizen, and transuniversal specialist, Sentace had convinced the administration to choose him for the assassination job, and gained a rare ticket off-world. Upon leaving his planet's confines, he'd discovered how *laughably* limited his knowledge actually was of multiversal economy, immensity, and key factions... such as the vast and infamous Casthen organization who now had his life in their grip. They and their mysterious leader, Çydanza, were applauded by some and despised by others. Their ethics were fluid. With one hand, they enslaved and monopolized and destroyed, and with another, they rehabilitated, cultivated, and reversed extinctions. Sentace scanned for clues about which of those hands had grabbed him.

"Ou, big 'uy," said a strange little creature in the cradle beside his. The words squished in their wide, froggy mouth. "You w' the weird eys. I c'n smell wha' you're. The spiiiicies." Besides a bandit strip of pink skin around their ink-drop eyes, and adorable parabola ears, they were all downy white fur. "I know wha' comes next. Wanna team up w' Chiidi? I love t' eat."

Before Sentace could respond, the bottom of the ship folded apart to reveal sky beneath everyone's feet. After hours of sensory deprivation, the view was a door to a dream.

Several prisoners shrieked. Sentace's calm dropped away with the floor. A flare of acrophobia spun his heart rate higher, and his restraints proved unnecessary as his muscles locked up anyway. It was a newfound fear since there weren't many heights on his planet and he'd never gone up to its orbital station. That had been the sole job of Evi Omai, their only pilot. If she really had sought asylum with the Casthen, was she now flying dropships like this? More rote routine, enslaved to another institution. He hoped she was sent out on multiversal missions, allowed all the freedom she'd incinerated a world to have.

He forced himself to look down. It wasn't a view he'd expected, and a low whistle of astonishment passed his lips when his breath returned.

The night side of this planet was skinned entirely in dark

megastructure, with emerald and gold pleochroism rippling across the surface. A web of lines and window lights scored it. There were enough Casthen emblems and colors to mark this as the faction's headquarters; the most closely guarded secret in the entire multiverse, impossible to reach. No wonder he'd been unconscious and veiled for the trip. This was a place that no one who saw could leave and live to tell about it. Lucky him.

The dropship banked, showing a ring of twilight ahead and the dawn of a distant, languid sun. Sentace choked down another urge to hurl.

"*Nine crimes*," someone swore, voice pitched high by terror. "Hundreds?"

"We're meat," barked the man with augmented legs. "Experiments."

"Now, now, be agreeable," said the xenid encased in the brain-pan of the mechanical skeleton. A vocal emitter parsed its speech into hollow units. The leggy creature splayed against the glass of its container. "Panic aids none but our captors."

Nice to know some of this crowd was reasonable. Sentace braved another look down to find out what was terrifying criminals as sordid and bloodthirsty as these. Twilight illuminated the planet's most surprising feature, one that Sentace's homeworld shared: the surface was blistered with variously sized bubble universes. Some universes scooped into the planet itself, trans-forming chunks of it, others hovered over the surface like dewdrops, and many stuck together into foam clusters. More must have been buried or encapsulated by the megastructures and ruins. A few universes were skewered by scaffolding and walkways and tunnels. Others, dangerous, were left well alone.

Every universe—whose sizes here ranged from fist-size to small moons—was a space that differed from others with unique changes in physics, as if stepping into a slightly different version of the world. The rinds that separated universe spaces were energy membranes allowing anything to pass through... though not always safely.

Someone quavered, "What in mercy are those?"

Another chortled at them. "Oh, baby thing, you are in for a *treat.*"

Sentace's heart skipped. This planet spelled death for anyone unfamiliar with universe bubbles. His home planet had thousands more universes on and around it than any comparable area of space he had learned of until this moment. This Casthen world had what looked like a hundred times more universes on it than Trow. With access to such a wealth of physical conditions, no wonder the Casthen were the heart of economic production, trade, and research in the multiverse, however profit-driven and immoral. And no wonder this Casthen stronghold's whereabouts were so sensitive a secret that even a whisper of curiosity voiced at the edge of a galaxy could bring soldiers swarming in, as they'd done to him.

There was clearly more environment than the Casthen could explore or use. Occupied megastructure had dominated the dark side of the planet, while out here in the light, ancient architecture was devoured by jungle and sea, giant mountain ranges, distant hurricanes, and plains of building-tall fungal growth. A morbid fascination bubbled over Sentace's fears, and even the dizzying height felt surreally interesting. A bird's view of nature reborn from moldering civilizations.

The crowd's reactions ranged from awe to dread. At the row's end, a musical voice sang, "Bringing us out here... must be a research project too gruesome to house with other operations. Rare physics translation tests, or the like."

Sentace was willing to bet on that. The prisoners hadn't been killed outright, so they were headed into forced labor or to be used as a material.

"Translation?" said the fluffy white xenid named Chiidi, beside him. They gaped at the view. Poor thing must be unfamiliar with how universes worked.

The ship slowed over a landscape of cratered hills, close enough to make out herds of animals fleeing through orange copses of scrub brush and quartz pillars. Sentace tried to relax his tense muscles before the restraints pinched circulation. Lightheadedness blurred the view. The hopeful part of this predicament was that, for now, he was still on Evi's trail, since she'd been headed to the Casthen and might be on this same planet's dark side. Once he sent home proof of her death—the Trowan administration wouldn't know if it was faked—he'd be liberated from his old government for good and able to disappear and start a new life.

A fully armored Casthen soldier entered from a door at the end of the bay. Their armor was strangely and intimidatingly mismatched, as if they'd torn the best off of everything, and instead of looking ramshackle they looked *optimized*. A smooth and mostly featureless mask in dark blue drew his eye up in ways he didn't want.

Sentace inhaled deep to raise his voice and lie that he was with Evi Omai and this was all a misunderstanding, but the crowd began babbling at the same time.

"*Shut it*," the soldier called, louder than the rabble. A material in their mask both amplified and deadened their voice.

Half the group quieted down.

"There's an energy anomaly, out 'ere, somewhere. We want it tracked." The soldier held up a finger-length device like a rod of faceted diamond. "You all've been given a touchstone. It'll glow the closer you get, and activates a beacon once completely charged. Set off the beacon and you've won. Winner gets to live. Winning's the only way off this planet."

Sentace glanced at the canyons passing below, dizzied by his fraying nerves. He breathed as deep as the chest bands allowed.

Winner gets to live.

The crowd rioted with fresh objections, to which the soldier added, "There can be only one winner, so don't get friendly."

The elder woman named Molinar hissed, "Asinine. Do you sincerely have no budget to find this anomaly yourself?"

Another, out of sight: "Nah, the anomaly's a lie. They wanna watch us kill each other."

More dissent heaped on. Most prisoners assumed they were going to be free-roaming test subjects. Sentace couldn't argue with that... he wasn't buying the setup of an anomaly interesting enough to seek out yet so uninteresting they would only use expendable resources to find it. He'd learned that the Casthen valued utility, could be heartless, that their operations often had little oversight from their leader Çydanza, and that they were rumored to engage in all manner of grotesque experimentation, treating bodies as raw substance.

Chiidi next to him stared at the forest below while wringing their tiny, spidery pink fingers. They murmured repeatedly, "My fur canno get *wet*."

The poor creature didn't fit with the rest of this trash. Neither did Sentace—he wasn't morally gleaming, but Trowan life was so tightly controlled, it had no room for crime. He asked, "How'd you end up here?"

Their ears flared and their fur puffed on end. "Blew it up," they squeaked happily. "Blew a lot of 'em up."

A tiny saboteur, this Chiidi. The likes of Evi, able to take radical action. Sentace warmed to them immediately. There was a whiff of smoke in their fur, the scent burned into his memory along with the fiery silhouette of Evi Omai. She stood atop the steps of administration, still wearing a pilot's neural halo around her head. She'd torn off her Trowan uniform, down to her undergarments, like shedding an old skin. Her hair was tied high in a long tail that reached her thighs, the mandated style for a woman of her age and position. She held it by the end, straight out to the side. A knife gleamed in her other hand as it sawed the tail short. If you're going to rebel, do it all the way, eh? Wind full of fire sparks caught the liberated strands and whisked them away along with the years of history they contained, the legacy of Trow up in flames.

The dropship pulled down to a lush green lowland. Flocks of birds exploded off patches of berry canes, filling the air with wings.

Chiidi asked in turn, "Wha's a chef doin' 'ere?"

As Sentace opened his mouth to reply, the passenger's restraints at the head of his row disengaged and the person plummeted out the open belly of the ship. Their scream dopplered as they swept past.

Oh. Oh shit, they were being *dropped* dropped off.

Sentace shut his eyes but that let the vertigo loose. Everything spun, which was worse, so he gritted his teeth and stared straight down, letting his vision soften into a blear of colorful texture. As gorgeous universe bubbles and clusters passed by, Sentace tried to convince himself this was like home. This was his element. He pushed panic to the bottom of his mind and hushed it under a swell of confidence.

Some distance from the first, a second competitor was released. They flailed, which made their body whip end over end.

The fall was a couple hundred meters at least.

One passenger was hooting, psyched up, loving this. Another raced through prayers at the top of their lungs. The skull-containered xenid with the mechanical body plumped a shock-absorbing material throughout its frame. Lucky.

Another release. They were going down the rows in order. Was it better to anticipate his turn, or not?

The next individual to fall was fully armored, but hit the domed membrane of a universe and incinerated while passing through, incompatible with the laws of physics inside.

No. Definitely better not to anticipate. Sentace's heart jumped, pulse throttling his neck. He unfocused his eyes again and breathed. The unlucky person's armor scattered to the swamp below. There was going to be a lot of luck involved from here on.

Poor Chiidi was next. They blinked a nictitating membrane over their eyes and trembled. The cradle opened with a snap. Chiidi's long, skinny arms flared out. Their clawed hands hooked onto Sentace's boots.

"Hey!" he cried while the xenid flapped beneath him, fur slicked smooth by wind.

Boom. Sentace's release was detonation. Metal ruptured around his limbs. All sense of the ship ripped away as Sentace entered free fall.

BEARINGS

Sentace tried not to be one of the ones who shrieked on the way down, but as the canyon floor hurtled into view, a raw sound tore out of him. Rushing air clawed apart his yell. Walls swallowed the light. His attempts to right himself only created spin as something heavy kept toppling his back earthward, and the spin dislodged Chiidi, who squealed.

His spine ruptured on impact—or felt that way. A pack attached between his shoulder blades burst into a plume of shock-absorbing gel. The explosion of compressed air pillowed beneath Sentace, but he was heavy, and still hit the ground hard enough to keel over. He groaned and curled up while the ultralight gel deflated with a pathetic wheeze.

In the quiet that followed, a bird chirruped as if he were trespassing. He made a note to find and eat its eggs later.

The roar of the departing dropship faded. Sentace caught his breath while the world stopped spinning. This air tasted dark and rich, moldering, like detritus and stagnant water. It reminded him of the old growth forests of home.

"Ouaaa. Alive," a voice crooned. Two wide-set, ink-dark eyes and a frowning line of mouth popped up inches from his face. Chiidi was waist height, small enough for the landing gel to have totally encased them. Their white fur swooped comically after the wind tunnel of the fall.

"More or less." Sentace rolled onto his ass, wrestled out of the gel membrane, and probed for injuries. There was no way the Casthen cared enough to calculate the maximum distance and speed each individual could drop from and survive. At least a few competitors must have died on impact, if they hadn't hit something unfortunate like that one fellow and the incinerating universe.

"Very squishy hume."

"Yeah, well, a lot of it is muscle, too." Most of Sentace's aches and bruises were from travel while stowed confined and unconscious until the dropship. His empty stomach stabbed him with pain, digesting itself. Dehydration, fatigue, lack of fuel, sluggishness... recovery was priority number one.

Chiidi did a whole-body shake to fix their fur, then stretched their arms. The wrists were joints on which a second length of arm hinged, with a translucent, veiny wing membrane stretching between. It looked paper-thin, vestigial. "Ancestors weep," the little xenid whined, "canno fly."

"Be grateful. I bet the Casthen would have cut your wings if you could."

Sentace dusted off his loose trousers and fixed the wrap of his modular tunic to turn it sleeveless. The atmosphere was cool, shaded, and muggy down here. Craggy walls formed a valley courtyard, the cracked-open remains of a facility reclaimed by forest and bizarre mineral growths. Walkways became streams, and streets turned to rivers. Distant waterfalls drained through broken ceilings. The light above looked like midday headed toward dusk. Perhaps first priority was finding a way up top for a better lay of the land.

He tightened his bandolier of spice vials and unsheathed his chef's vari-knife, which had held up beautifully. Different edges made it knife, saw, hook, trowel, and firesteel, all in one. Crude compared to diamond edges and flame teeth and laser this-and-that, which he couldn't afford, but his knife's metal retained its qualities in most universes where other technologies failed.

Chiidi plucked at an object tied to their ankle: the touchstone that, the Casthen soldier had explained, would light up in response to the anomaly. Chiidi experimented biting it.

Sentace had one too, around his waist. He broke the band and tossed the touchstone in the river. "Probably a way to monitor us."

"I 'ave no skills, but c'n smell and *pi pi pi* hear things." Chiidi wagged their ears. "This no emitting signal."

"Yet."

"If we throw 'way," Chiidi argued, "and 'nomly *is* real, we 'ave no way to win."

A lose–lose gamble. Keep it, only for it to transmit to the Casthen, or ditch it, only to have no way to track a genuine energy signature.

"We can steal someone else's if we find proof this isn't just a kill game."

"We!" Chiidi threw the device over their shoulder while spreading all their fingers into starbursts of glee. "Then Chiidi come w' you. Safe 'n 'ave own private chef."

Sentace chuckled, but his spirits dropped. The last thing he needed was more dead weight like the louts who had gotten him captured in the first place. He'd need to feed them both, now.

His mouth watered as he mentally put together a pan fry of game meat, wild onion, river cress, and diced mikonut cheese, tossed with steamed parro grains and wrapped in a whipped egg covering, garnished with crackling skin and chili crisp. His restaurant's cultural administrators would have never sanctioned such barbaric use of an egg.

Sentace picked a way through the broken streets and canyons. The place seemed city-vast, but most materials were decayed, and electronics corroded. He gathered a few pieces of scrap metal for later. At a frigid stream, he washed his face, raked his fingernails across stubble, and did his best to detangle the dark, shaggy hair that brushed his shoulders now. A strand of grass served as a tie at the nape of his neck.

Chiidi skirted well clear of the water. Their back legs were short, feet flat and wide, their gait an all-fours scuttle. They bounded to a nearby universe bubble one meter across and off the ground at knee height—or shoulder height for Chiidi. This universe's energy membrane rind of delicate light looked bluish and irritated, and the interior oddly murky, giving Sentace a guess at its properties.

"Careful," he warned. "You're not familiar with universes, are you?"

They shook. "None on Chiidi 'ome."

"Your biology might be incompatible, so don't touch any rinds unless I tell you it's safe." He could only guess at Chiidi's exact makeup, but transuniversality was key to how he cooked. This rind's prismatic hues twisted in a heat haze shroud. Beyond that veil, pebbles and liquid droplets floated inside the universe. Gravity looked funky, but at the macro level it would be safe enough for human flesh. Chiidi's, maybe not.

Another large universe sphere bifurcated the building's upper levels with a rind of gentle flux. Interior physics turned the stone into a porous matter in which jewel-like mosses thrived. Ahead, a few small universes stuck together like a foam while half submerged in the river, turning the water gelatinous in one and clotted with algae in another.

Sentace's planet's universes weren't this close together, and it was rarer to find them fused, but the familiar sight put him at ease. To the other competitors, they would be dangers rather than opportunities. Maybe the environment would take them out before they got in his way.

Universes nested within one another and comprised the fabric of space, impossible to move or destroy. The energy rinds of their borders were like permeable curtains. Matter could pass through, but would be translated to fit the unique physical parameters inside that specific universe: Sentace's entire culinary specialty was transuniversal physics, how ingredients would transform between universe bubbles. Material reality was continuous and the landscape one continuum, but within each universe's space, the laws of physics diverged in ways that could be inconsequential or catastrophic. Most people needed a measuring device to determine a universe's temperament, but Sentace had experience and a few cheats he'd invented.

He plunged his hands into the bluish universe. The rind's energy yielded through him. Fractals chewed each other apart on a microscopic scale. The blue color rioted into a metallic purple. His skin tightened uncomfortably inside the universe, bloating to where he could feel his pulse.

The skin of his hands and forearms were covered with indicators: an assortment of pigments, chemicals, minerals, air pockets, and particles that reacted to universal parameters. An inked hycus flower's willowy petals on his inner wrist turned luminescent cyan. The stem shrank and grew powdery. Crashing waves bled red while the foam, a subdermal crystalline material, started to tickle. A line of metallic dots changed refraction, like a code. While turning his arms back and forth to see everything, Sentace puzzled the reactions together into an overview of this universe's physical laws.

"Ou!" Chiidi exclaimed. Their ears perked. "Cool. Brave."

"Only the brave get to discover new things." Suspicions confirmed about the universe's nature, Sentace picked handfuls of golden river algae nearby, then plunged them inside. The fibers spiraled and the physics compressed them, making oils bead up on the strands. He filled an empty vial. The oil had a soft, oceanic aroma.

"Something like this could happen to you if you cross the wrong rind."

"Ouaaa." Chiidi's mouth gaped, exaggerating the natural grumpiness of their features. Their wide-set eyes and downturned jaw reminded Sentace of a bat. Chiidi asked, "Your world 'ave many?"

"Very. My kitchen was built around eight universe bubbles, big and tiny." Sentace checked a few more indicators on his knuckles before passing a flat piece of metal scrap into the rind. The material softened to a rubbery consistency that allowed him to press it into a pot shape before removing, where it hardened once again.

Chiidi wiggled their fingers. Clapping?

Sentace continued, "My society didn't use a tenth of the universes available to it. A massive waste of potential, like everything Trowan. They focused on a few rare delicacies produced through transuniversal ecology."

Trowan society was a monoculture built solely around these agricultural exports and related tourism. Deviation from the mold was punished. Creativity was a sin. It enraged him to think about a planet with so much diversity cloistered and tunnel-visioned for centuries on just a few trade goods. Not even regular citizens were allowed to venture into the wilderness without an express role involving it, like Sentace gathering ingredients and utilizing universal alterations.

"Del'cacies like wha'?" Chiidi asked.

"The bark to make caqeña, a stimulant drink. The grass for Luster, a liquor. And opilla, an expanding grain that's an affordable food for impoverished worlds."

"Opilla puddin!" Chiidi's arms shot up. They fanned their twiggy fingers. "I love."

Sentace patted a vial of grains on his bandolier. "Stay out of trouble and I'll make some."

"You now Chiidi's fave hume." They scuttled along while leaping out of the way of every puddle or water drop. They couldn't get wet, they'd said.

Sentace remembered something else: "Chi, what did you mean when you mentioned you knew what would come next?"

" 'Ave been captive 'ere long time." They stretched their chest tall and smoothed a hand down the fur so it lay flat, revealing the lines of a brand: the Casthen insignia, which looked to Sentace like the circle of an eye seen from above, with six rays shooting out beneath. All-seeing: gathering information and dispersing control. Reminded him of Trow. "Other ships w' pris'ners go out, come back empty."

Well... that didn't answer whether the anomaly was for real or if there was an experiment afoot.

"How'd you get captured? For blowing up Casthen property?"

"No no no. Captive 'fore that. I blew up thing *here*." They emitted a creaky sounding giggle before turning serious. Or was that just their neutral face, deadpan and grumpy? "Am iredimi. Rare xenid. Soft soft *soft* fur is pyrophobic. Big monies. Casthen cornered the market. I think..."

They slowed their pace as they worked feelings into words. Sentace busied himself picking wild onion and piquant green herbs.

Chiidi shivered then continued, "Good Casthen killed poachers on iredimi world. Keep us safe. But take Chiidi 'n others. I think Casthen breed us."

Another silence followed. Sentace let his remaining questions float away. Chiidi probably tried to escape by exploding something.

" 'Nomly must be special creature," Chiidi mused. "Casthen always gathrin' special things, like iredimi."

If the anomaly was a creature, it could be on the move, which might explain why no one had found it yet and why the solution the Casthen had arrived at was to scattershot hunters across the landscape.

Sentace investigated a tree and the questionable kelp-like egg purses hanging from its limbs. He clipped one for later. The familiar rhythm of wildcrafting lifted his spirits above his exhaustion, and a dish took form in his mind. He followed a scent and found a bushy plant with savory, peppery-smelling red fruits that would stand in for the vegetable he wanted. Testing their surface oils against the toxin indicators striping his left arm, he deemed them safe.

"How you 'ere?" Chiidi asked. "Chef poisons Casthen! Lock 'im up."

Sentace had poisoned a minister years ago, but no one recently. Chuckling, he said, "I volunteered to hunt down a fugitive on behalf of my planet's government. They needed to make an example of her, but their own xenophobia made them balk at hiring an off-world assassin. I was the most likely person to be able to navigate the multiverse, so they agreed to let me leave the planet."

"Chef 'sassin!" Chiidi barked in excitement.

Sentace snorted. "I'm not going to kill her. She galvanized me and a lot of others—if anything, I'm seeking her out to thank her."

A few times in his life he'd taken his feelings into his own hands like Evi had done, and broken Trowan edicts in a radical way. But his acts had been secret, quiet. Meek, compared to her daring catastrophe. His acts had been drops of poison, not mountains of fire.

He stopped walking as the overgrown facility finally terminated at the mouth of an unusual mountain range. Peaks bowed onto the landscape with clustered stone planes jutting randomly, as if the ground had been snapped from different angles. It formed a vast, broken cavern with sun rays slanting in through the strange frames of rock. The scale was difficult to parse. His visual confusion echoed back to the fire Evi had set, which he'd first glimpsed from the lowland center. Looking up at the hills, the scale of the inferno had been horrifying, impossible to make sense of.

"Wha'd Evi do?" Chiidi prodded. "Story's juicy. I c'n tell."

"Evi was our planet's only pilot, transporting tourists to and from the orbital station. That made her one of the only citizens to witness that view and realize what a fishbowl our world was. An idealist. She wanted freedom for everyone and new possibilities after generations of oppression veiled as order and tradition. Forced ignorance is a form of imprisonment, I heard her say once."

A low purr of appreciation rose in pitch up Chiidi's throat. "Revlution'ry lady pilot. Ver' cool."

The Trowan system had been toxic, slowly killing off its citizens through a combination of mental illness, burnout, and disease. Most people snapped inward, taking their own life, but Evi had snapped outward.

"Very cool," Sentace agreed. "Anyway, there was no way to start a revolution, so she burned it all down."

Chiidi's mouth stretched in horrific glee, their black eyes

glittering. "Whole planet?"

"The opilla and lustergrass fields. The caqeña forest."

Her coppery ship had flown unprecedentedly low and torn away from its mandated flight path, over the settlement. The engines blasted a ferocious sound that thundered within the valley. Fuel dusted from the underside of her ship's wings and dewed on the vegetation. Then ignition sparks had rained down.

"After, she exploded the orbital station. It plummeted to the surface in pieces, taking out everything critical that the fires hadn't. All Trowan industry, destroyed in a day."

Citizens had died too. People Sentace knew and liked had been lost along with all the parts of his world he'd been delighted to see burn. The life he'd invested in—his whole identity—had been destroyed on that day, and as much as it had suffocated him, it was all he'd had. The rage he'd felt was still there, like a base note flavor, but he couldn't bring himself around to the idea of killing Evi, because admiration was part of him too.

He concluded, "My assassination mission was supposed to be solo, but I got a handful of people looking over my shoulder to make sure I killed Evi Omai. She made contact with the Casthen, then disappeared. I assumed she sought asylum. My incompetent associates poked the wrong Casthen network. I was captured as a result."

At least he was also rid of those imbeciles now.

Once he found Evi—hopefully back at the Casthen's head-quarters on this planet and not galaxies away in the wind—he could unlink himself from his old life for good. He could watch from afar as Trowan society failed to rise from the ashes Evi had made of it.

First he needed sustenance and bearings. This space was a huge crescent-shaped arena framing a single large universe that had all the signs of being fatal. He would bet his knife that this had been a sacrificial place. Fat trees shouldered their way through the stone floor, and the ones closest to the deadly universe curved unnaturally to avoid it, forming a bizarre cage of limbs. They looked climbable to the plateau of the facility's roof for a lay of the land, as long as he didn't fall in the universe below.

As Sentace walked, a scattering of razor light hit him in the eyes and his mind registered a bolt of shiny steel coming at him.

"*Crimes*," he swore and ducked. It was a universe the size of a pearl. If its physics didn't warp light, he would have walked right through without seeing it and put a hole in a heart or lung. Chiidi, hip-height, had walked right under.

He called these mini fatalities "bullet hole" universes. Fetching his second piece of salvaged scrap metal, he passed it through the caustic rind to disintegrate the material and carefully shape it into a spoon.

"You're so *cool*," Chiidi crooned, admiring the utensil.

Sentace stacked a tower of rocks beneath the universe so he wouldn't walk into it later. He asked, "Do you know how to make a fire?" Something to put the iredimi on task and cut off the deluge of questions.

"Chiidi is firestarter like Evi." The little iredimi bounded off.

Finally alone with his thoughts, Sentace's mood grew heavy. This planet wasn't home, and even if Evi was here too, she was half a planet away, and his companion was a liability, however adorable.

He let focus erode those feelings: cutting fresh shoots, soft tubers, and wild onion into perfectly tiny cubes... struggling not to fall back into Trowan perfectionism. The cuisine he'd served to tourists and ambassadors had to be cut identically to the millimeter. Nothing could deviate from traditional preparation. Certain ingredients only, to be treated in the sanctioned way.

Crimes, it felt good to start speaking of that life in the past tense. Thank you, Evi.

He'd been able to endure the rigidity of the restaurant because catering to tourists was a loophole through Trow's isolation and xenophobia. He'd experienced different species, heard stories about the multiverse, and discovered new perspectives on food and traditions around eating. It had stoked a curiosity for more.

Sentace turned to the trio of clustered universes, their rinds fused. One was head-sized, one big enough to hold Chiidi, and the last was two meters in diameter and submerged into the floor, making a pit out of the stone. He ran his hands and arm around each, watching the indicators and mentally constructing a sense of the character of each bubble.

The new puzzle energized him. He passed the savory red fruits through the smallest universe, which shriveled them as if they'd spent days sun drying. He then swept them straight into the lower universe, where the seeds jiggled out to the skin and exploded, coating everything in effervescent dust. Then into the last set of physics, where the fruits rehydrated and softened.

Sentace mashed them into a paste while Chiidi returned and built a fire. He heated algae oil in the makeshift pot to sauté the vegetable cubes with some spices. A splendid aroma started to release.

Chiidi looked on in wonder, finally awed silent. They cuddled up to the fire, where their fur puffed enormously, proven fireproof.

Sentace interrogated Chiidi about their diet. Iredimi biology was close enough to patrons he'd served before from distant worlds, so he settled on a fish stew: light but fortifying and comforting. It would hydrate them and had ample protein, carbs to restore energy, herbs that would aid fatigue, salt for Chiidi's low blood pressure, and fats for healthy fur. The fish were easy to catch by hand, and Chiidi had never eaten one before, given their species' aquaphobia.

Stock and fish meat went into the pot to simmer. A pinch of chili flakes dissolved into tiny bubbles and tinted the dish red.

"Watch," Sentace said as he stepped to the trio of universes while spearing a hole in one corner of the tree-hung egg purse he'd picked. At the top of the largest universe, he dangled and waved the egg in a circular motion. The whites flowed out and fizzed as they passed the iridescent energies of this rind. Within the bubble itself, the viscosity increased, turning the flow into one long noodle lightweight enough to levitate within. Sentace coiled it up, cut shorter strands, and whisked them back into the pot. They cooked into a fluffy texture with air pockets that absorbed the broth. Another sacrilegious use of an egg by Trowan standards.

"Ouaaa!" Chiidi looked on with huge, glistening eyes. Crimes, this creature was growing on him, but he really didn't need the burden of companionship.

"Put this yolk over there." Sentace nodded aside. The red yolk inside the egg purse smelled greasy and would overpower the fish. Chiidi scuttled away and squeezed the yolk out. A troupe of lizards slithered over to feast.

Sentace divided the stew into two halves of a hollowed-out fruit that would lend it some acidity. He used the smaller universe to foam up drops of algae oil for a garnish, then sprinkled a fragrant, citrusy green herb on top. The milky broth had a sheen of oil and chili, and the rough chunks of white fish contrasted with the three-texture diced vegetables. This was not a Trowan fine dining dish. It felt good to play again.

Chiidi's fingers wrapped their bowl's entire circumference, with one claw hooked inside to guide morsels to their mouth and slurp. They gradually puffed up with pleasure and increased core warmth, as if rubbed with static.

Sentace chuckled and took a gulp, pleased the stew tasted as intended. The soft fish flaked, the tender tubers matched with the delicately crunchy shoots, and the broth was hearty but light. Bright herbs and citrus lifted the fishy flavor and nutty oils, with a hint of spice elevating the warmth of it all.

Strength recovered, they could scale up and assess the landscape, then he'd ditch this "competition" and seek out Evi's trail at the Casthen's main megastructure, a quarter of the way around the planet.

"Eat up," he said, mostly to himself. "There's a long way ahead."

COMMENCE

Sentace and Chiidi finished their meal to soothing echoes of insect percussion and birdsong. Bowl empty, Chiidi rocked back, belly distended—after *three* servings. A resource hog as well as a chatterbox.

Chiidi's damp white fur had dried and puffed, looking unbelievably soft. No one would believe they'd endured a harrowing experience and had an uncertain future ahead. Food nourished body and mind. Being cared for soothed the heart.

"You know," Sentace mused, "I heard that Casthen soldiers eat bland, grey, mealy nutrition blocks. No wonder so many of them are assholes."

"Casthen who save iredimi from poachers: also asshole."

Sentace packed the remaining ingredients, filled a makeshift bladder with boiled water, then experimented storing coals in the rubbery egg purse.

Chiidi's ears twitched. One pinned back to the river. "You think pred'tors in thi—"

A brilliant streak whistled between the trees. On instinct, Sentace flipped the stew pot in the air. It received the tunneling energy at an angle and spun off sideways.

Chiidi shrieked and scurried up the nearest tree. Sentace snatched his vari-knife before scrambling behind a different tree. His heart pummeled his rib cage, and all his clear-headedness fogged. Another competitor, this soon? He shouldn't have gotten comfy in the first place. Idiot.

A second shot plowed through the tree trunk by his head. He flinched and gripped his knife tighter, as if a chef's knife wasn't shit at this distance. All Sentace knew about multiversal weaponry was that offensive and defensive devices were called glaves. By the sound and color of the energy traveling through this universe, and the spiral char mark around the strike, he guessed this was choreon-based ignition. A good idea pierced his mental haze.

Before fear robbed him of action, he sprinted to the extremely dubious cover of the universe cluster he'd been cooking with. A volley of shots chased him. One exploded at his feet while the final one blasted the largest universe, slowing as it dragged through the blurry veil of the rind. The physics translation within contorted the spearhead of energy into a puff of warm air by the time it reached the other side and hit Sentace in the face.

He buckled in relief and tried to stop hyperventilating. Thank all the moons—choreon was incompatible with this universe. He centered himself behind it.

The shooter fired a test shot that fizzled out again. They arced sideways, and Sentace matched their walk, keeping the two-meter-diameter universe shield between them. His view was blurred by the rind's fusion folds and ethereal magnetism, but after a moment, he recognized this human from the dropship. Two augmented legs—maybe even fully aug, no flesh at all, judging from the gaps in the frames. They were bent in an animalistic design, with high-end materials and synthetic muscle, except much of it had melted, causing jerky steps and lockouts. Must've found out the hard way that not all universes play nice with augmentations, especially the fancy ones.

The man clicked his teeth. "The inked-up one who fell with that white bat."

Guess Chiidi resembled a bat to others, too. Sentace replied, "And you're that guy I don't know or care about, who has no reason to kill me."

He couldn't decide whether it was worse to have to fight or to make an alliance and gain more dead weight. Viewing the man's face through two wavering universe rinds wasn't doing it any favors, but it was the face of a life that had started bad and got worse. The man's skin was scarred, drug-pitted, solar-damaged. Waxy black paint circled the top half of his head through short-shaved greying hair. He was shirtless, shredded, with shrink-wrapped skin: undernourished and dehydrated. That plus the compromised augs was a stroke of luck. Sentace was well fed and he was desperate to win, so he would.

The man said, "Didn't you hear? This is a test."

Interesting—not a game or a search?

He wagged his free hand at his waist where three touchstones dangled. Two trophies of the dead. "Nothing personal."

Alright, there was no talking this out. The killer now stood two meters from the universe's edge. Sentace backed up and angled to put a different nearby universe in range: a huge bubble arcing into the sky, with its bottom at nearly head height. He filled his palm with two spices from his bandolier and shook his fist to mix them. This would take careful timing. *Breathe.*

The killer's legs made a sudden *snap* of power. He sidestepped around the universe with augmented speed and tracked Sentace's mad dash away. Sentace barely dodged a shot while flinging his spice mix across the bottom of the incendiary universe above the two of them. It was meant to ignite and rain fire... except he'd gotten something wrong. Half the mixture dusted over the man's head and shoulders while the rest smoked into a great cloud.

Sentace's dive out of the way landed him on his side and knocked the air from his chest. Two blind-fired shots missed him by inches. The man fanned the smoke away and aimed his next shot properly while Sentace scrambled to get up.

A screech yanked the man's attention away. Chiidi had leaped from the treetop, wings spread in an awkward glide. They crashed into the man's head while dumping the egg purse of embers in their grasp. It ignited the dusting of incendiary spice.

The fireproof little iredimi clung on and fanned the blaze with frantic wingbeats. That waxy shit in the killer's hair and across his face must have contained grease because it whooshed into greater flame, further oxygenated by his flailing about. More smoke spewed, and the sulfur stench of charred hair filled Sentace's nose.

Chiidi was heavy enough to unbalance the man as his leg mechanics locked up. Sentace seized the opening and dashed to close the distance. With no clear target on a thrashing opponent in a cloud of smoke, Sentace stabbed at his torso but clipped an arm instead. Hopefully an artery, from that gush of red.

The killer howled and grabbed Chiidi, whose claws dragged over his neck as he threw them off. Chiidi was so lightweight they swooshed across the clearing and crashed into the river.

"*Chi!*" Sentace bellowed. The *water*.

The killer shot at close range. Sentace sidestepped the flash on instinct. He grabbed the man's glave-wielding wrist with one hand and stabbed with the other. His own wrist was grasped in turn—just as he wanted. With superior strength against this lean opponent, and taking advantage of the stuttering leg augs, Sentace walked him backward to the universe where the glave shots had fizzled out. With a powerful twist, he tackled the man's glave arm through the rind.

One shot got off first: it seared across Sentace's skull above his ear. He screamed and heard the sound of it suddenly muzzled, followed by a ringing blur. At least the universe wrecked the glave. The ammo inside was incompatible with these physics. It transformed into an acid that burst the chamber open and melted a couple of the killer's fingers as a bonus.

Sentace scrabbled for his dropped knife and received an aug-powered kick in the gut. His lovely stew nearly came right back up.

Then a *click*. The killer's knee locked out at the apex of the kick. Sentace yanked his other ankle and toppled him.

Adrenaline tasted rancid but was blotting Sentace's pain. He rolled up and plunged his vari-knife into the skinny killer's abs. A jerk snared organs with the knife's hook.

The man roared. His aug leg notched back, knee bending—so fast, the sound felt like a blow—ready to drive at Sentace's chest.

Barely thinking, Sentace tore the brightest vial off his bandolier and smashed it in the attacker's burned-raw face. The mix of citrus and capsaicin produced a vile sting, and elicited a shriek that Sentace was glad his blood-filled ear couldn't register.

Woozily, he *did* register the tower of stones marking the tiny bullet hole universe, several paces behind the killer.

Sentace rose, feeling bigger now. He let the man get up, too. What a wreck, that face. And those fancy legs, pushed to their limit.

"Sorry, I guess," Sentace said huskily as he swallowed his pain... crouched... and with as much explosive power as he could muster, tackled the killer one last time.

The man's torso pitched back and upward into the tiny bubble. An awful splitting sound carried through his chest cavity. Bone cleaved. Blood spurted. The pearl of annihilating physical laws passed into his neck, clavicle, and one lung.

Sentace collapsed with the effort, landing halfway on the other man. Breathless, hot, shaking, head pounding, he made himself fetch his knife again. He knelt grimly over the spasming body, ready to finish the job.

There was nothing to finish. The corpse's muscles twitched as it bled out.

Sentace watched in a daze. The blood cooled on his fingers. This wasn't his first time killing... but it had never been this visceral. He wasn't a fighter. And yet, with his old identity burned alongside the Trowan crops, he felt raw, ready to be pressed into a new self. The path to Evi was changing him.

His sense of control sank out of reach. The familiarity of the landscape washed away like a layer of paint; the shape of the plants, the scent of the soil, the colors of the light... all foreign. Hostile.

The three touchstones glinted on the dead man's belt.

At some point, Sentace's breathing had slowed to a stop while shock worsened his shaking and filled him in with chill. Pain oozed through the new fissures in his sense of safety. The blood from his head wound covered half his neck and leached into his shirt. Then a thought swooped in and hit him like a whack to the skull: "*Chiidi.*"

Whimpering, he shuffled to the river. On the bank lay a bright white, soaking wet mass.

"Chi." Sentace fell to his knees and reached out. For a heartbeat, no response. Then Chiidi gripped a few delicate, shivering fingers over Sentace's hand. The poor thing could barely function.

"I killed him. It's safe for now."

No answer.

Sentace swallowed. His head was swimming, cognition bobbing around. "Are you... Does water hurt you? Talk to me, little guy."

A long pause followed before Chiidi unfurled and emitted a few burbling squeaks.

Their fur was impossibly waterlogged. Sentace resisted the urge to press on it. "You've got half the river in you, eh? Does it damage iredimi, or...?"

"No," they sobbed. "But'll take *weeks* to dry. Weeks!"

Sentace wanted to laugh, but Chiidi's voice was so broken, and water continued to sluice out of their mop of a body, his heart lurched instead.

Chiidi looked up at him. A nictitating membrane ran over their eyes and blinked away water that resembled human tears. Sentace doubted iredimi cried—most species did not.

He said, "You heard that guy coming before I did. Good ears. Can you walk?"

Chiidi's ears flicked, throwing off water drops. They made a pitiful attempt to move their legs, as if they weighed several hundred pounds now.

"Can I carry you?"

A nod. Crestfallen ears.

Sentace picked Chiidi up, enduring a drench of river water that came out under the pressure. It washed some blood away, at least. He returned to the camp spot and gathered up their supplies, then blotted clean water at his awful, tingling head wound, which seemed less catastrophic than during the frenzy of the fight. The blast might have cauterized it? A swipe of hair had singed off, the skin felt ugly, and the tip of his ear was gone. He emptied a vial of liavon from his bandolier and sprinkled it over the wound to stanch the blood. Good enough for now.

Finally, he trudged over to inspect the dead man's body. Having spent his life hunting and butchering, the meat and blood didn't bother him. Anatomy was clinical rather than grotesque. He told himself it didn't matter that the shape was human. It looked the same as any other opened-up creature.

There wasn't much to pilfer: some metal components from the augs, some fluid sacs, some small knives barely worth taking.

He left the three touchstones. If the killer hadn't been compromised from those two fights and however many universal crossovers, Sentace would not have survived. Thank you, whoever these two were.

It was sinking in now... that the idea of a winner-takes-all death match was real to some of these individuals, even if Sentace didn't believe it. He wished he hadn't destroyed the man's glave.

"We need to get moving, Chiidi." His pulse hadn't normalized, as if a countdown was racing now. He gazed up at the flat ridge, which looked reachable by climbing the big trees that bent around that fatal universe at the arena's end.

Chiidi gave a weak whine as Sentace picked them up. He got drenched again. Chiidi wrapped their spindly arms around his shoulders and burrowed their waterlogged head against his collarbones, and grumbled, "You scare me."

"I know." Once more, Sentace mulled over the dark, raw feeling of having become someone different for a moment. The professional, sedate veneer he'd worn for his work all those years was peeling away. "But I kept us safe. Hold on."

SCOPE

Atop the plateau was a new landscape of squiggly, striated mineral in huge pluming arcs, the geology born from some explosive event. Sharper outcrops flowered out of the ground in bursts, and Sentace questioned if they were actually organic or petrified. Among them rested gigantic hollowed skulls and fossilized jaws and rib cages from long-dead megafauna. Tree canopies peeked up from canyons and busted-open substructures. Pockets of grassland held herds of animals, mere specks from here, and ancient buildings encrusted faraway mountains, hazed blue by the distance.

Bubble universes dotted the view in all sizes, from kilometers wide to bullet holes. Hard terrain to navigate. Entire directions could be cut off if it meant crossing over into somewhere unkind.

Sentace found the sight daunting. This planet felt paved over and over, colonized and toppled and recolonized. A palimpsest. He couldn't tell how old the architecture was or in what style. The Casthen's leader, Çydanza, had been alive for unknown centuries, so these could be Casthen buildings from ages ago. With so much under Çydanza's command across the multiverse, Sentace wouldn't have been surprised to learn there were operations she'd forgotten and left to rot.

Or it could be civilizations that predated the Casthen. For all he knew, these were Graven ruins, built by that species so ancient they drowned in myth and legend, their remnants scattered across the multiverse: mysterious technology, multidimensional architecture, the stellar egresses to wormhole across distances, and faint traces of their genetics. Many believed that the Graven had created the multiverse in the first place, as the only beings capable of manipulating the fabric of the cosmos in such a manner. Perhaps it made sense that a planet littered with universes like this had been a home of theirs, eons ago. And if their remnants were here, it made some sense that the Casthen and other civilizations would have excavated and colonized it in this manner during their searching.

Sentace perked up at a stroke of luck: there was a tower in the direction of the sun, several hours of hiking away. The spike-shaped structure glistened, looking brand new in this landscape of ruin. The top flattened into a ring encircling a bubble universe that the Casthen obviously studied or used. At best, the research tower would have computer systems operational, maybe even a crew or a ship. At worse, it would be a great vantage point to look for other opportunities and plan a route to the Casthen's main operations.

Chiidi grew colder in his arms. He questioned how robust their circulatory system could be with so many veins in those paper-thin wings and ears. Chiidi wasn't going to make the trek to the tower, and a bank of storm clouds blew their way. Sentace poured his energy into exploring universes in between, while watching his back and sticking to cover. He was a big, easy thing to spot, and Chiidi was bright white in the gloom.

In his daze, Sentace wondered if the Casthen were watching. Was a satellite catching the show, and a monitor somewhere showed blinking spots for all the touchstones in play?

"I think that's a good candidate, just ahead," he said, though Chiidi had fallen into a grumpy stupor and mild hypothermia. "See the rind's flux is fuchsia edged in metallic green? The transparent counter-ripple chevrons? This one will dry you."

Hopefully he sounded soothing. People had commented that the purr-like masculine undertone to his voice was intimidating even when he spoke gently.

Sentace picked his way down a hillside and stopped where the universe domed out of the ground. He whooshed an arm through. Moisture hit him first, like a second rind of mist clinging to the border, and his arm came out dewed with water. The inked flowers snaking around his elbow sizzled bluish, but the stars of nordinean quartz encircling his wrist remained dull. Nodules of chemicals above his knuckles changed in solidity and refraction. Sentace compiled all the indictors into understanding and, satisfied, he walked in.

Chiidi groaned as they crossed the wall of vapor, but beyond it the universe became warm, pleasant, and homey. Outside sounds grew hushed while a few lone insects stridulated, the clicking of their legs falling in and out of rhythm. All the foliage changed to sunset hues and smelled heat-baked, like resins and warm spices and rising dough.

"You can hunker down here. Not for *weeks*, but..." Until Sentace had a stronger plan to get to Casthen headquarters.

A cluster of giant flowers anchored to the rock like succulents, with stiff, waxy outer petals and more layers within. One was as tall as Sentace and twice his height across. He set Chiidi down and sawed an opening into the flower's empty, dried-out center, as good as a closet-sized room.

Chiidi did a whole body shake, which made their fur stand out in spikes. "Warm," they approved as they scuttled inside.

This wasn't a fantastic universe for Sentace—his heart was already palpitating, muscles working harder, oxygenation compromised—but he could endure for now. To avoid drawing attention, he lit a fire with smokeless fuel and used a ring of swelterstones he'd been lugging just for Chiidi. They would absorb heat and radiate it for hours.

As the space warmed up, leggy red insects squirmed from between the petal walls and flattened across them. Shiny, frilly appendages flew open on their backs. Sentace drew his knife, but after a beat of quiet he realized the creatures were simply using organs to reflect heat as they swayed. Harmless thermophiles.

Heaviness left Chiidi's fur and made it clumpy. The crown of tufts atop their head made their wide-set eyes and huge frown all the more surly. They peered at him warily now. "Sentace is kind t' Chiidi, but kills like killin's normal."

Sentace thought that over as he dabbed his head wound with an acemannan gel he'd scraped from a lucky plant find. "Kindness and ferocity can coexist in one person. I guess you can say I'm kind to good people, but relentless to the vile. Is that scary?"

Chiidi scrunched up and pulled their ears down. "Chiidi'll be good."

Maybe food would repair this. Sentace started to cook up a stockpile of snacks. His own wories vanished while he was cooking, where all he had to focus on was bringing out the flavor. He made opilla pudding sweetened with a creamy sap. Marinated lizard, grilled. And a stack of savory things made from squishy nuts that he discovered exploded into crispy tendrils when fried.

He stepped outside the universe to ensure the fire's candescence wasn't visible, then covered the flower entrance and curled up inside to sleep for the first time since the Casthen had electrocuted and abducted him, days ago.

Sentace's dream started at home. The opilla and lustergrass fields were aflame, making terraced mountains of fire. There was only one way to evacuate from the rift valley, so the population flowed in one throng, a river of confusion and sorrow. Sentace trudged the opposite way, seeking out reason, until he saw Evi standing atop the steps, her figure branded upon the ruins. The sight was unreasonable. Inevitable. Exhilarating.

His dream crumbled into glances of imagery as it raced through the time that followed: Sentace volunteering to track her down, arguing his case hard, desperate that she would become a hero and not a martyr. Then the multiverse, a havoc of newness through which he chased the familiar... purchase records with her name, footage of her shape, descriptions from strange species who all saw her a different way. The dream turned frustrated and surreal, devolving repeatedly into a fire on some distant world, as if she were a pattern destined to repeat.

Evi's silhouette dissolved in the flames, never to be caught. Sentace woke with a start, his sinuses filled with fragrances of flame, of heated stone, of ash. Blinking away sleep and pulses of a headache, he realized it was his own fire. He fed it the last of the fuel.

Chiidi slept upright like a bird, arms folded and head scrunched down, feet tucked under fluff. Drying well.

Sentace stretched, prepared a few more food items, then gathered his equipment and ingredients. He left the pilfered knives. Chiidi was safer staying in here than with Sentace, and if more fights were inevitable, he didn't want to have to worry about a companion as well. Besides that, foraging and cooking for two—especially a bottomless stomach like the iredimi—would make travel far slower, and having another species along limited what universes could be traversed.

This was for the best.

As wrong as it felt to leave without a better goodbye than the extra food, Chiidi needed rest and Sentace didn't want to see the glint of trepidation in their eyes.

In case Chiidi was listening, he said softly, "I'll try to come back for you."

COMMON GROUND

Hours of hiking difficult terrain was far easier without having to worry about the sun setting or the temperature changing. Either the days were excessively long, or this planet was tidally locked. He guessed the latter... and how lucky were the Casthen to possess so many universes and constantly stable conditions?

From a summit, Sentace spotted what he guessed was another competitor at the valley's base, on the run from a pack of two-legged beasts that were three times their prey's size. The individual dodged through thickets and ravines, but was stumbling and losing ground as the pack fanned out to cut them off. Exhaustion, dehydration, and malnutrition were formidable enemies too.

A snap of low, tonal sound thundered through the valley and ricocheted off the mountai sides. Sentace jumped. It wasn't thunder—too short, too *round*—and the figure being chased suddenly exploded into pieces. The predators were on the feast of remains in a heartbeat. Had they created that deadly sound somehow? Or it was a glave, and another competitor in the distance had taken an easy kill?

Sentace huddled in cover, planning a new route around the valley. He snacked on vitamin-packed fruits until he felt the danger had passed, then he continued on, falling back into familiar isolation, meditating to the rhythm of steps as he outpaced the rainstorm. Thunder snapped at his back and startled him, but this was real thunder: the deep, choppy kind, a crack that seemed to split dimensions and roll the contents out across space. Rain curtained the distance in grey. Chiidi would be fine. Even if the water-wicking universe filled with moisture, the bud walls were a good roof.

By the time Sentace reached the base of the tower, the landscape had changed from volcanic plains and valley oases to crumbled stone and metallic architecture now overgrown and fauna-infested. The research tower sat on industrial megastructure that caverned deep into the planet. Sentace found the entrance below ground. The utilitarian surfaces were painted in years of weathering and developing ecosystem. Moss cladded the iron and stone. Glossy blue mushroom caps peeked out of wall seams, and bowed floor panels had become puddles filled with luminous micro-organisms.

Sentace's pulse jumped as he spotted the rectangle of light marking the elevator door. Electricity, in this neglected landscape, felt like water in a desert. The rails of the door unknit and slid into the frame as he approached. The floor lit cheerily as he stepped in, and the door closed. The lift ascended on its own, to the top, nearly two hundred meters up. Sentace pressed his spine against a solid wall and fought the urge to shrink into a corner until it took him back down.

The door opened to the base level of the observation ring,

revealing a window wall wrapping all the way around the ring room. Lightly hyperventilating, Sentace stepped out and gaped as he forced himself to look. A swooping feeling dropped to his stomach, half from the height and half from the futility of the sight. The Casthen's facilities glittered on the far side of the planet beyond mountain ranges, a small sea, glaciers, leagues of darkness, and countless universes. Beady lights of ship traffic swarmed the surface. The distance felt like twice the breadth of Trowan wilderness.

Even with his skills, it looked infeasible to cross without finding a creature to ride or a usable vehicle with enough fuel to cross the barren stretches. He would waste away on the journey, without a purpose, all his capability put toward nothing in the end.

Sentace's mind went numb and his focus unhooked. He drifted around the ring. The opposite view was of ruined megastructure and desert sand stretching to the bright side of the planet. Organic growths—fungus?—sprouted from the distant architecture, as big as buildings themselves.

He spotted flashes of weapon fire roughly ten kilometers from the tower. Some of his opponents would have the same idea about this place. Making haste, he found a ramp to the middle level, which wrapped around the base of the universe in the center. Dust collected on an array of fascinating lab equipment: gossamer probes, phase-changing crucibles, tanks of alien botanicals in preservation gel, hybrid organic-mechanical arms that reached from wall to rind, bottles that contained auroral-looking substances, and more. Voids on shelves and in test containers suggested the Casthen had taken their experiments back to the main facility.

A cage wall separated the ring room from the spherical universe. Its thick rind was nearly invisible haze, wavering, with inner snaps of light and shadow that resembled prominence erupting off a sun. Sentace could already tell it was tremendously dangerous and worthy of building a tower to reach.

Accepting that his own curiosity would get him killed one day, he stuck his arm through the cage as far as he could and spread his hand, still a good half a meter from the rind's edge. Bumps prickled across his skin, which grew hot, the water in his flesh threatening to boil. Every indicator on his arm and hand responded: the inked substances, the chemical nodules, the embedded metals and gems... put together, they painted a gruesome picture of what this rind would do to a person. This was the sort of universe where almost nothing could cross over to the inside, even if it could exist *on the inside* just fine. The rind was too violent, as if it changed a thing to its opposite and back again and again, flickering it into nothingness.

Sentace retracted his arm and scratched at the deep itch around his bones. "These Casthen have so much. What I could do with a fraction of these resources..."

His whole life had been spent speccing so hard into trans universal effects as his expertise, he felt useless for any other career at his age. But in the right space, freed from the confines of society, community, and organization, he could make a name for himself. Become renown. Not only in cooking: with just a short amount of time experiencing the multiverse, he could now envision his knowledge applied to medical issues, material sciences, species relocation, starship engineering... Food was a means of healing and communicating, and he saw the potential to do the same for a whole multiverse of peoples.

If he survived.

Sentace pried his gaze from the deadly bubble and found the ramp up to the third and last floor. He was greeted by fully powered consoles glittering in the dim room. A grateful swear hissed through his teeth. One of these systems could have Casthen headquarters intel, travel sheets, or communication hubs. At the very least, he might wreck something important enough to bring ships over to investigate.

He turned the curve of the room. The rind's fluid rays slicked over the gunmetal surfaces and filled the air like veils. Amid them, a silhouette shifted.

Sentace unsheathed his vari-knife and stared while his vision adjusted.

The tall woman hefted a massive glave onto her hip, two meters long, all complicated rails and chambers. Surely a long range weapon. Sentace recognized her as the elderly woman named Molinar whom the other prisoners had been harassing in the dropship. She'd had the demeanor of a powerful leader. Golden jewelry weaved through her hair and throttled her neck. Metallic paint sketched sprays of flowers across her dark face and caught radiance, winking like the starry consoles. She was Sentace's mother's age; similar wrinkles charting her leathery face, long coils of black hair fading to white, and the tired, no-bullshit resolve of a woman who had raised up the world alone. Sentace fought off an instinctual softening.

Beside her, the console was frenzied with information modules and code mid-hack, a connection to the main systems open. An emblem Sentace recognized blinked in anticipation: she was accessing remote communications.

As his pulse rocketed and tension seized him up, Sentace raised a placating hand because what else was he going to do with it against a sniper glave, even at close range? "Molinar. I don't intend to play whatever this game is. I want to get out of it, and it looks like you do too." Straight to it. He wasn't "negotiation tactics" kind of smart. This would be the mental version of his knife against her sniper glave.

"Certainly," she replied coolly, "you do not look like you belong here." Molinar's voice was low, gravelly, and strong, and her tone gave no quarter for argument. A voice accustomed to command. She hadn't tried to shoot him through the rind as he walked up the ramp, so she was smarter than the last guy. Instead, she backed up to gain the range her glave needed.

This woman was intelligent, armed, connected, and skilled at hacking. Teamwork was a fast-track to new problems, but right now, Sentace really did need someone like this.

He started, "Let's—"

"Why should I?" she interrupted. "You want to cooperate, but what value are you to me?"

By careful centimeters, Sentace angled himself in front of the consoles, hoping she wouldn't shoot in the direction of her salvation. She didn't seem to notice—her one mistake. "I'm a transuniversal science expert, a hunter, and a culinarian who knows how to survive in landscapes like this."

Molinar flicked something on her glave. Milky, featherlight gels blossomed in layered, lens-shaped pockets along the barrel. Power hummed at its core. Sentace went rigid. He thought back to the competitor running from the predator herd, who had been exploded into pieces by a thunderous sonic click. That had been Molinar, sniping from this tower.

She raised a perfect eyebrow. "Once I reach my people, I can leave this place. So what *are* you to me, dear?"

What value was he to someone like this—or to anyone—if she didn't need the skills he'd poured all of himself into? "I'm useful to you as an extra body. More hands, more senses on watch, someone to soak up attacks. I'm stronger than you, and strong is useful."

He couldn't get the blinking communication symbol out of the periphery of his vision, where it shouted how close an escape route was. If Molinar closed the system, he would never get it back open.

Thunder cracked outside, close. The instruments and loose machinery in the ring jittered. Humid, ionized air clung to him atop his sweat, which began to trickle down his face.

Molinar leaned both ways to get a look at him. "I have never seen eyes in your colors, but I know that look in them. A solitary creature, spurning connection, unwilling to bend around others. You do not *want* alliance, you would not be subservient, so I am afraid you are not trustworthy nor worth my time nor the air in this room."

Molinar's tone triggered something in Sentace's core. Her personality was quite Trowan: strict, no inch given for disobedience. The way of enduring people like this was engraved in Sentace's being. You cave in, bow, let the boots tread upon your spine. He wasn't going to be that person anymore, wasn't going to leash himself to anyone or anything. She was right—he didn't want this.

"Are you any different from me?" He couldn't stop the quip once it flowed. The tension between them approached a boiling point. "I imagine you're surrounded by company, but solitary and unconnected and unbending at the top."

That was the Trowan way: the governing body had control, but commanded no loyalty. The system functioned, yet devoid of creativity.

Molinar's face contorted in a snarl, removing any resemblance she'd had to Sentace's mother.

He rose up taller upon seeing her poise could be broken. He ventured, "I can tell what universes are safe or not. You're going to need that to reach the anomaly."

"The energy anomaly is a technology," she said, "something that has come online deep in one of these facilities. A weapon, most likely, and one that *I* will claim, though not by wandering around in the dirt."

"Then there's no point in killing me, either wa—"

"The point in killing you is to eliminate a variable I do not have time to interrogate or manage." Molinar lunged sideways for a clear shot. The glave's membranes bulged then vibrated. In a hideous *snap*, blur enveloped the glave and Molinar's figure.

Sentace ducked against the electronics. A blast of sonic energy cannoned by, putting thunder to shame. The click shot missed him, but the proximity waves blistered into his ear canal on the injured side. Pressure crunched into his skull. With a pop and a stab of pain came silence, ringing, compression like a heel grinding his head into the wall. He yelled but it was more sensation than sound, a strangled vibration in his throat.

Part of the damaged console burst into shrapnel and sputters of electricity.

More pops, above him. *Bolts.* The sonic blast had hit the ceiling near the bubble universe. Bolts resonated at the shot's frequency and flew out like bullets, turning to puffs of dust as they pierced the universe rind. The metal rods they'd held formed a dome over the universe, with a tall finial at the peak. The entire structure buckled on one side and plunged into the universe, which chewed the copper down.

While Molinar gaped at the destruction, Sentace sprang to close the distance. His vertigo worsened, spinning the room beneath his feet. Ringing noise hashed between his ears, and wetness dribbled from both. He collided drunkenly with Molinar as she hauled the glave up between them—it was too heavy, and so was Sentace. They toppled to the floor, her unbalanced and him dizzied.

He flipped Molinar's useless rifle from her grasp and straddled her, reaching for her head. Her mouth opened in an O but he couldn't hear whatever scream she made.

He said, "I don't need to ki—"

Molinar gripped his right arm, locked his right leg, and in one smooth motion, bridged and rolled him over, reversing their positions. He grappled with her awkwardly as she kept him too close to get any hold or leverage. Fatigued and inflexible, he was making gaps big enough she could slip through.

Sudden radiance burned the room. Pressure waves exploded into Sentace's chest, and Molinar fell off him. The room spun again as he watched debris glitter down. *Lightning.* It was a lightning protection structure that had been destroyed by the rifle blast. The storm crouched over the tower, bruise-black and vicious.

Sentace dashed for his dropped knife. Molinar rammed him weakly but enough to double him over the console. A second shove with her whole body toppled him over the rim of the ring. There was no cage wall here.

With the deadly universe roiling half a meter past his back, Sentace scrabbled against the wall until he caught the cage of the lower ring. Two hundred meters of air plunged beneath him, the landscape smeared by terror and vertigo. Dangling, he snapped his head upright, looking anywhere but at the height. Fits of lightning spidered through the clouds.

Molinar's head appeared over the rim of the level above. She hefted the sonic click rifle.

"*Don't!*" Sentace bellowed. The cage didn't have an opening he could see, and a panicked kick didn't even rattle the metal. There was nowhere to go but fall.

Folds of gel blossomed over the glave barrel while Molinar

47

aimed it straight down.

Sudden flashes branched from the heavens—not from her shot. One lightning arm connected to the tip of her rifle. Another blasted through the universe rind. The entire bubble blazed with light, its insides beating molten radiance, electricity boiling, before the universe lensed the lightning to skewer straight down the elevator shaft in a tight beam.

Sentace smashed himself against the cage wall, clinging for his life while a ferocious heat seared his back. Thunder detonated in the universe core, sending concussive waves through the ring rooms. Part of the cage tore open, and Sentace immediately scrambled to it, strength superhuman, fueled by a desperation to feel solid ground beneath him. He hauled himself inside.

An explosion rocked the platform. Glancing over the inner wall, Sentace confirmed his fear: the elevator shaft's base was a crumbling mess of fire, cables, and shorting electrical conduits. With his eardrums burst, the scene lay eerily quiet beneath a muted, ringing pressure. Pieces of structure detached and drifted, growing small. The floor beneath his feet tilted.

"Crimes, what do I keep getting myself into?" He sucked his pain back with a hiss. Adrenaline helped carry him back up the ramp to the top level.

Molinar stood at the console, clutching one arm and navigating glitching displays with the other. She swiveled to snarl at him.

Sentace ignored her. The ceiling—there was an access hatch and footholds at the outer wall. He sprinted for it. Molinar screeched behind him, but he didn't look. She could die. Not his problem.

The observation decks began free fall, tilting so the rooms' inner sides passed through the universe, where its flux gnashed the steel and spat out dust.

Sentace shouldered the hatch open and crawled onto the rooftop. With a great shudder, the tilt worsened and the universe sheared off a quarter of the structure. Sentace braced so he wouldn't slide straight into the universe's maw.

Thunder split the sky overhead and rumbled through Sentace's body. The sensation grounded him. Calm. Focus. A vista of cloud stretched ahead. His entire being resisted looking down, but he made himself tally the universes available to jump to.

Molinar slithered onto the roof, clinging on her belly. Golden fingernails snapped as she death-gripped the surface, forty-five degrees tilted now. She yelled, but he heard only snippets. "— jump? Where?"

Now she was desperate for him. They had both lost control of the situation. He spared her a final glance over his shoulder. "You look like you've never had to pull yourself up from the bottom before."

Blood reddened the teeth of her grimace. She climbed toward his feet. "I will allow you on the rescue ship."

Molinar had ended up here for a reason. *Retribution.*

Sentace said, "You had your chance to bargain with the better me. I'm not actually a good person." He kicked her hand, dislodging her grip, then stepped to the rim of the platform as it tilted past forty-five. Molinar slid out of the periphery of his vision.

A running jump wasn't possible and there was no time to calculate. Sentace fixed his gaze on three universes beside the tower, two hundred meters below. It was jump or die. A wrong universe might even be a faster death. His brain shrieked at him to curl up, hold on to solidity, hope for the best. Rebelling, he charged along the rim and *leaped.*

His stomach heaved to his throat. The world yawned beneath him. Wind plowed up for the second time in the last few days, and he started to lose his mind. Senses unraveled. He swam his arms back and tried to bullet his body toward the large blur of a universe doming over the canyon below.

Sentace struck the rind and immediately felt a flash freeze sensation, his skin prickly and itching. Panic razed his nervous system, making him flail while he crossed over and the temperature equalized. Gravity inside the universe bucked against his fall so hard he was sure bones broke. A force like whitewater rapids flipped him onto his back and side, stopping his fall... but not letting go. Instead of passing through and being slowed enough to survive the fall, he was stuck entirely.

A fresh slam of panic made him vomit. Threads of stomach acid splattered along bizarre gravitational lines. Trying to follow their flow, he wheeled his limbs, heading down to the bubble edge while the universe core clutched him like a bug in a fist. His fingertips scraped the rind, stirring its fractal foam.

Shrapnel from the collapsing tower razored into the universe and stuck too, eddying in gravity wells as its lethal speed slowed. In a flash of self-preservation, Sentace balled up, letting the worst of the debris get snared.

His lungs were squeezed so tight he couldn't get a thread of breath. He bucked until he could kick off the broad side of a suspended girder. It was enough to push him to the universe's base and then out: falling again, gasping, swearing, headed to a second bubble universe that bifurcated ground level.

Crossing this rind was like another punch in the gut. Gravity was normal, meaning the remainder of his velocity threw him against the dirt. The wind knocked from his lungs... which was bad because this universe had no oxygen. His throat and eyes parched. Blood crusted over his ears. Electrostatic charge made his hair stand on end, skin hot and tingling. His chest throbbed as he dragged his body, beyond exhausted, to the rind's lucent haze.

As soon as his torso crossed over, he sucked in a huge breath and expelled it all in a yell of frustration and pain and relief. He lay out of the tower's radius, a riot of dust and debris and crashes pummeling the layers of old facility at its foundation.

"Mercy's tits," Sentace wheezed, the curse barely forming. "No more heights."

He groaned and let his head fall back. Grit crunched in his hair. The ringing in his skull had stopped but an aching pressure remained. The storm front carried on to a bright horizon, laughing in fits of lightning. A few raindrops spat on his face.

Far-off past the storm, a speck in the sky gleamed as it changed course, headed for him.

WINGS

One ship was inbound. Molinar had mentioned a rescue ship, but not that she had made contact in the end. It could be a Casthen vessel rerouted to investigate the explosion. The tower might even have had a remote alert system.

Sentace sat by the wreckage and wasted precious moments just breathing. His head felt underwater. His sweat chilled. His shoulder had taken the brunt of the fall, and felt one jostle away from dislocation. He thought of Chiidi cozy in their warm little universe many hours away, and nursed a pang of jealousy.

If Sentace could hijack the incoming vessel, he would save months of travel across the Casthen wilderness to freedom and Evi's trail. Most ships had decent autopilot. He would also have room to bring Chiidi and a cache of supplies.

The ship was everything he needed, but with the way his luck had been going, he wasn't betting it would land nearby. There had to be a way to catch it. A bird in a net. Given that the tower systems had been active, there was a chance a nearby facility might be similarly powered and perhaps have weaponry or an electromagnetic pulse or the like. If not, he'd have to work with whatever lay in the kilometer of overgrown, multi-level mega-structure between the tower and the ship's straight course. That was all the ground he had time to cover before it arrived, judging from the rate the speck was growing against the horizon.

Sentace stared while his mind unhooked from his brain, too weary to rummage up excitement for this fresh challenge. His entire body was battered and broken, and a shadow slipped over his heart. The Casthen landscape—a wild world mid-rebirth—had been novel and exhilarating at first, but now felt thoroughly *foreign*. He'd murdered, and abandoned. He was part of this "game" whether he meant to be or not. His Trowan identity was shedding away, and he couldn't tell what new thing lay underneath. He'd even lost his vari-knife, which had been with him his entire career... such a small thing to shed, but with it something integral had gone.

With the tower's hope crumbled to the ground, he now he had to catch a bird out of the sky, without tools or supplies. If he could get it to land, somehow, he would feel his way through what came after.

"Get up, you piece of shit," he muttered affectionately as he bullied himself to his feet and gathered the shards of his former desperation. "Don't lose until you've lost."

The terrain ahead was the megastructure's roof interspersed with jutting planes of carved stone as tall as hills. They disintegrated gradually into a hazy desert that marked the blazing center point of the planet's tidal lock. A glistening band of silver suggested ocean. There were no more forests or much plant life ahead, but farther off, the largest growth of fungi he'd ever seen engulfed the architecture, spewing from it, dwarfing it, breaking it down with the weight of massive cerulean florets and lacy caps. It was too far away to tell if they were living or desiccated.

The clouds released rain just as Sentace found a way into the underground facility. He inhaled lungfuls of petrichor fragrance and scrubbed some of the raindrops over his face to slick back his hair. "Hang in there, Chiidi."

If he were honest, he missed having that little iredimi along for banter.

The underground lacked electricity, clogged with darkness except where ceiling cave-ins admitted light and rain. Dirt had blown or washed inside over time, giving substrate to anemic vegetation and networks of ghostly mycelia. The bioluminescence of plants and small amphibians cast an eerie emerald mood through this underground night.

Raindrops on metal, and the cold, crystalline sound of trickling water joined the percussion of purrs and insect chirps. The megastructure felt lonely and funereal even as it filled with sound. Chasms revealed tiers stacking into the earth like mines, and straightaways stretched kilometers across the planet. Storage zones branched off, most emptied of goods and deformed by the voids. Old machinery lay rusted, overgrown, cracked open.

With every new room, cavern, and corridor, Sentace saw industry, the interrogation of nature, and ecology bent to economy. The stories of this place had become too large, too ambitious, and crumbled into a rotting catacomb of failed or abandoned endeavors. He imagined an alternate future of what his planet might have become if it hadn't been so aggressively segregated from the predatory organizations that would have exploited it. On the one hand, it had been protected from abuse like this. On the other, its potential had gone undeveloped for centuries. Sentace couldn't decide which was worse.

One giant storeroom held a cerulean fungal species resembling those far-off ones that had grown big enough to subsume the facility. These crept from rows of vats that had cracked open as time swallowed this place, breaking them in the throat of history. The fungus had escaped... or perhaps colonized and fed on something else in those vats? The fruiting bodies were luminous white with blue ribbing and a blush of magenta, linked together by a network of spectral roots that explored beneath the floor and bulged it up with more growth.

The mushrooms absorbed moisture where rainwater dripped on them through ceiling cracks. Sentace picked one and found a thicker stream to hold it under. Instantly it expanded three times in size. Membrane puffed between stretched gills. The water that rolled off had a static-like shimmer. He investigated the other waterlogged fungal patches and noticed the same shimmer in the fluid that trickled away, a glittering of spores or electric dendrites seeking connection between colonies. Could they share resources that way?

"*Hmm*," Sentace hummed, and sorted this discovery among everything he'd learned. Like a recipe, he needed the right ingredients. The correct method. A way to get that ship out of the sky intact.

Sentace took the mushroom with him for a light source and rain canopy. As he rushed down a long concourse, the rain became a downpour, forming streams along the lane as it filled the facility. He added flash flooding to his list of fears, and picked up the pace. He also discovered a limit to how big the plucked specimen could expand without a nutrition source.

The concourse ended in a courtyard large enough to hold several starships, carved through the middle of a rocky hill, with an ornate vaulted ceiling that still held glass after all this time.

A stench hit Sentace immediately: decomposition, but also bright and chemical, almost pleasant. He shielded his nose and investigated the house-sized universe resting in the courtyard's center. The mountain had been hollowed around it. Inside lay animal carcasses, new and old; all types. Scraps of skeleton were so aged they had mineralized, and flesh had turned to fertilizer while atop rested lumps of rotting flesh, creatures Sentace couldn't make out with the body parts blended together.

The carcasses encircled a small pool fed by a spring of the most gorgeous water Sentace had ever seen: a lustrous lavender color filled with flinty particles that caught the light and sparkled. These creatures had come to drink.

His gut said to move on fast, but there could be something usable here. He passed his arm through the rind and noted the warning swirl inks lighting up. Flecks in his palm turned silvery. This universe compromised circulatory systems slowly enough that you could die, unsuspecting, while visiting such a watering hole.

Getting an itch of idea, Sentace tested his other arm's indicators to confirm more specs. He stepped in long enough to plant his mushroom into the corpses, and watched the hungry stem entangle the tissues.

"That's it." He peered up at the old glass ceiling that rippled grey with the roar of rain held back. "The recipe."

He was out of time and alternative ideas, in any case. None of the facility was as serviceable as he'd hoped.

Head high, Sentace jogged back to the vat storage room full of fungus. It could communicate and propagate by water. Sentace poured his effort into making the room exceptionally leaky, which turned out to be a good frustration outlet, too: he pounded holes in flooded walls, climbed up to pry at ceiling panels, and hauled debris out of the way to make the currents he wanted. He harvested an armful of fruiting bodies, then marched back to the courtyard while kicking rubble away from the glittering stream coursing along with him. His steps were haunted by the distinct feeling that he was loosing something ancient that should have stayed in that room. Oh well.

Back in the covered courtyard, his rivulets connected with the carcass piles. Fungal life rooted ravenously, a white lace exploring the layers of remains. The colony migrated through the water, stitching this new area into the old. Sentace planted more fruiting bodies and marveled at the sprawling network crossing the borders of body, water, electrostatic, dust, and what else? In an impressive swarm of coordination, the fungus dominated the mound of nutrients and flowered several meters tall, but Sentace splashing rainwater on them was never going to be enough. He had the right species, the right universe, and enough fuel, but needed the ignition.

Dashing onward, he sought an access route to the surface that wasn't clotted with wreckage and vegetation. He emerged on a rain-slicked roof. The distant, gigantic fungi that were digesting the facility gave him hope that his plan was viable.

Twilit clouds backlit the starship incoming. It looked small, unable to fit a military squad, and sleek, like it wasn't another dropship of convicts. There were no obvious guns to its silhouette, though Sentace wasn't betting on being that lucky. Altitude, too hard to judge... half a kilometer high? Maybe much less. Its low course avoided the universe bubbles at higher altitudes. Sentace mentally calculated the intercepted time if its speed remained constant.

"This really isn't sane," he admitted aloud. Madness felt good, in fact, after a life and career doing only the sane and sanctioned.

First, the glass ceiling over the courtyard. Sentace fetched a long bar of scrap steel. He grinned as the ends of his mind snapped into alignment, finally. Transuniversal change was a rare expertise, he was in the best location to exercise it, and he was in his prime: if he couldn't pull this off, then his confidence had been arrogance all this time. The dangerous unknowns of this foreign place were reviving a life force in him that he hadn't realized his repetitive Trowan life had hammered down so very hard. The future was uncertain. Time had meaning and teeth. Growth was a music, a rhythm of action and recovery.

As he'd hoped, time had wearied this glass. It was both warped, pooling the rainwater, and weak, succumbing to the slam of his makeshift hammer. Cracks skittered through the biggest piece in the center. Sentace jumped back in case it all went in one go. Smaller segments at the edges caved in at the shock, but he needed the middle to release—with timing—over the universe and his patch of mutant fungus.

Sentace kept his gaze on the ship. Storm clouds curled in its wake like reverent hands, baring a halo of sun glow from beyond. Salvation, that black bird.

He counted aloud, feeling calm despite his heart banging his chest and his fatigue turning inebriating. All his injuries faded out of focus.

One more blow and the thick glass changed its pitch, high and bristly. He scraped water off his face and positioned himself on the starburst of cracks near a support beam.

The ship torched over the megastructure, *so* close now. It veered once in a way that almost made Sentace panic. This plan failed if the ship didn't maintain course or if his timing—like cooking—wasn't precise, late enough that the vessel couldn't evade, but early enough that his net would reach the right height.

"Please let this work." He added a string of swears, muttered in melody like prayer: a childhood habit from Trow.

One. Two. Sentace jumped in place. The ceiling splintered beneath his feet along with its pool of water. He grabbed the support beam and dangled, but wasn't prepared for how slick the metal was. One hand slipped, and he swung, forced to look down. Water crashed over the carcasses and bones and glowing mycelial network, followed by the steady torrent of rain.

The mushrooms exploded in size. They swelled with absorbed fluid, pumped it through their roots, liquefied the rot, and *cl*. With a noisy crackle, giant caps bloomed skyward over a hundred meters, strong enough to curl aside the steel of the ceiling frame. Sentace's grip failed, but he fell onto pale fungal flesh as it burgeoned up, pushing him past roof level. He had enough sense to roll off and get clear as the rest of the glass gave way.

His view filled with warped membranes of surreal tissue as the fungus fanned toward atmosphere, the gills stretching into a net that pulsed with light.

Sentace gasped a breath that tasted of rot and smelled like bittersweet almonds. Dazed by the immensity of the reaction, he almost missed the roar of an engine. He whipped his head around to see the black starship roll sideways to avoid the wall blooming in its path. Its blade-like wings and vanes pulled in to slim its profile, but it still clipped hard into the distending fungal body. The roll turned into a bizarrely soft crash, slicing the luminous matter like a handful of knives. Out of Sentace's sight, the ship continued to smash, jets struggling to blast through while avoiding collision with the mountainside.

Those sounds were hopeful. Sentace exhaled. Then the glass beneath him gave way as another mighty bloom punched out of the courtyard and toppled him. This fall was cushioned, for once.

7

LUCK

"Nine crimes, I made a monster." Half a meter of silky white root networks covered every surface of the courtyard, networks upon networks, grasping the walls and infiltrating the ground. The fuzzy carpeting gave off a ghostly candescence. It squished under Sentace's boots, as if he were treading on buried bodies below. "Oh, that's nasty."

The air was alive with electrostatic now, making the small hairs on his body stand on end. Even with his muffled hearing, he could make out the frizzle of organic stress as the fungus continued to guzzle water and grow. It would eventually exhaust its new fuel source and stop expanding, but the rain wasn't letting up yet and the runoff carried glistering spores to other areas of the facility. What would they find?

Sentace couldn't shake the feeling that he'd done something

heinous. He'd mixed ingredients that would become the Casthen's problem in the future, whatever it cooked into.

Before he left the courtyard, he picked up a sliver of ceiling glass that was knife-wide and arm length. He fashioned a handle with a strip of torn cloth—far from a new chef's knife or cleaver, but he felt better with some kind of weapon.

The outer sheath of mushroom tissue would make a good rain cloak. He sliced a section to peel. Instantly the mushroom bled a pearly liquid. Exposed to oxygen, the droplets divided, again and again and again into a mist. It didn't resemble spore dust, but Sentace held his breath anyway and abandoned the idea. No reason to mess further with this monster.

"Rain it is, then." Sentace found a mountain tunnel headed upward. Runoff made it a river, and a roaring sound grew steadily louder. He hurried back outside only to see the fungus stretching too high to climb. Tears and scorch marks riddled one side. Sentace scaled the easier facility exterior until he had to climb the tissue wall itself. His glass knife and a sharp rock worked as climbing tools if he held his breath against the vaporous blood.

There it was: the ship had tried to bail to a vast drainage plateau cut out of the mountainside like a shelf. Luminous fungus folds had buffered the ship's crash as they grew. It had landed with its nose plowed onto the plateau shelf and its back half on the tissue.

And here was the roaring Sentace had heard: giant grooves in the shelf channeled runoff to the sheer cliff face, down to an ocean below. The flash floods he'd worried about were funneled here.

Through the rumbling white noise, he couldn't make out any voices or sounds of activity. Maybe the crew had died in the crash. That would be the best scenario for him.

The ship's glossy exterior was badly scraped, but it didn't look so damaged it couldn't fly, which was the genius of using an organic net to slow it. Sentace's heart continued marching, but all in all, this had gone better than he'd expected.

The vessel was long but not considerably wide, with a pointed nose that angled back to two main wings pulled against the body. There was something avian about it and something insectile. Most of it was foreign black metal, angular and sleek, with muscle-like strips of materials unfamiliar to him: pleochroic gels and shapely translucent alloys and arrays of layered plates that resembled gills. Sentace wasn't a hardware guy, but he couldn't help admiring its aesthetic. In any case, it looked fancy enough to have an auto-pilot system.

The back of the ship lay open in a whorl of jagged folds, a few of which connected at the ground to make a ramp to the inside bay. No movement, though it was dark inside.

Sentace crouched behind a frill of mushroom and quickly scanned the landscape for other competitors who would have seen the ship or the fungus. This vantage wasn't great. The best he could do was hurry. Cautiously.

He shed his drenched tunic wrap and tied his supplies inside, then stashed it. His soaked, flopping trousers he cinched tighter. The rain was frigid against bare skin, but it helped his focus.

"Okay." He straightened his spine. "Go."

Down the slope of the fungus he crept, then he crouched at the ship's side with his ear against the hull. No sounds. Two heartbeats, five, six... he skulked to the back ramp with the glass knife in a white-knuckle grip.

Please let there be only corpses.

Sentace sneaked up the ramp. The interior was one big bay that tapered to a cockpit alcove and a single pilot's seat, all dreamily lit by commingled twilight and bioluminescence. No crew. Contents of storage containers and wall compartments spilled across the floor. A sharp ramp scooped down in the middle of the bay to the darkness of a lower floor.

Shit, maybe the crew had bailed in the time it took him to climb up here. The ransacked supplies resembled a hasty retreat. If they'd left because the ship was busted, then this place was just a magnet for the other competitors.

Sentace strode to the cockpit. Blood spattered the seat cushions and the console. The holosplays were offline and the instruments dark except a few idle indicators in unfamiliar languages. He pressed the symbols he recognized, and the main unit lit up... rather glitchy, but he expected more warning reds if there was a problem. The engines were in the belly, which seemed like a weird design.

He swiveled back to the bay. A murky lump in front of him registered as an animal, and he froze a moment too long. The crouched figure lunged. One palm struck his jaw while something rammed his shoulder. His neck whipped sideways with an awful torque. Before his vertebrae could snap, he thrust the glass knife at his attacker. It skittered across the person's neck and cheek as they dodged.

Instead of retreating, they immediately grabbed Sentace and pulled him in, jarring his balance. As he stumbled, they twisted his wrist to try to free the knife, but his wits returned. Bigger and stronger, he shoved his attacker back.

Shadow-drenched, they were impossible to define except as human with female proportions. Punches flew at his face so viciously he could barely keep his arms up to block. He wheeled an elbow at her temple, which sent her staggering into the bay wall with a scream.

Pulses filled up his skull. Rain drummed on the ship's hull into a thick, consuming pressure within. His focus narrowed and he moved with killing intent, the glass shard arcing like a cleaver, cuing the muscle memory of butchery.

His opponent ducked and rolled by his legs, taking a skimming blow to the back that ripped her shirt. She sprang up close to his chest where he couldn't act and hauled his knife arm in a circle so it crashed into the wall. The weapon broke in half with a *clang*. Sentace managed to hold on to the serrated half as his opponent kicked his bruised hip and threw him on his ass.

He slid all the way to the ramp outside. A good idea hazed together in his mind. Crouched as if to charge her, he backed up to the ramp's edge where it met mushroom. Behind him, he dragged the broken glass through the tissue. Balls of fluid swelled out of the cut.

His attacker hefted a wrench the length of her arm and rushed him, dark and wrathful. Sentace dodged the blow and kicked up the bleeding drops in the same motion. Oxygen bifurcated them in rapid bursts, creating a pearly mist that reflected light. It blinded both of them, but he was ready for it. He slashed at the woman's neck. Glass screeched across the wrench as she made a lucky block, but the weapon jarred out of her slick grip.

Sentace yanked her to him while jabbing at a neck artery. Halfway there, her foot whipped around his ankle wicked fast and took him down. The glass shard bounced out of his hand. The woman toppled too with his added momentum, and their combined weight squeezed more blood from the fungus as they landed. Puffs of mist erupted in swirls, obscuring everything.

Sentace's muscles were burning for oxygen now, strength failing, and his attacker was clearly the better fighter. All he had was size, and it didn't feel so helpful anymore. He wrestled her to a supine position, pinned her, then pulled back a punch to finish things.

The woman heaved up and locked her arms around his neck. In smooth motions her legs wrapped his waist, her feet planted on his hips, and she thrust away from him. One of his arms she kept hold of, which straightened under excruciating stress. Alarm blared in Sentace's brain. He twisted around before his arm dislocated but she matched his movement and clung on to his back. Her arm barred across his throat, clamping in a choke hold, too much leverage for him to escape.

All damned, she was good.

The swirls of mist cleared around them. Static still raged in Sentace's skull and eyes, blood thundering, tongue sour, ears ringing with pain again. He heaved to a standing position, but that didn't dislodge her. Out of ideas, Sentace threw himself backward onto the ground, atop her with his full weight.

She just *took it*. Her arm around his neck didn't budge. Sentace's vision went milky. Lungs burned. He gurgled on a scream and clawed at her forearm.

She replied by pushing the back of his head into her choking arm, cutting off his airway.

He fumbled, unable to pry her off. The indicator inks and embedded materials in his hands blurred in his watery vision, making a strange mural across his visual field.

The woman's head was close enough to his that he could feel her breath against his ear and the incredulity in her whisper when she said, "The *chef*?"

Promptly, Sentace blacked out.

8

AGREEMENTS

S entace regained consciousness lying on his back. His hands and feet were bound with some kind of spray-on adhesive, likely all the woman could manage in the seconds his unconsciousness had lasted after being choked out. There was some give when he twisted, the fibers pliable while still drying. He stretched them but otherwise kept still. She could have broken his neck, but chose not to.

After everything that had happened, he felt pulverized and rolled out and folded back into the shape of a person. Mental processing was sludgy. He wriggled on the ship's ramp until his head was under the bay's overhang and out of the rainfall.

His attacker stood by the cockpit. The slant of twilight lit her bottom half. She was tying a knot in her shirt, joining the two halves he'd slashed apart. A thin slice had reached skin, barely deep enough to draw blood. Next she threw on a piece of outerwear he recognized as a morphcoat, which adapted material and shape to the wearer's needs and moods. As it settled around her frame, it slicked from puffy feathers to a thick black leather with a rain-proof reptilian sheen. She fixed her hair in a high tail off the top of her head, then settled a pilot's neural control halo around her skull, the thread-thin ring of light hovering at forehead height.

So, she was the pilot, but was she the *only* crew? Blood streaked down her lips and chin—that was why the console had been bloody. She'd smashed her nose in the crash. The blood on her cheek and the bruise blooming at her temple were Sentace's doing.

He blinked water from his eyes and looked again as her silhouette wavered over his memories, matching up to the image branded by fire into his mind.

"*Evi Omai?*" He choked on a laugh and let his head thunk down. The cool metal sobered him. This planet had some strange gravity that brought errant people and objects together. He'd heard once that the Graven's world had worked that way eons ago: synchronistic design. If they had inhabited or used this planet long ago, was there some remnant strangeness about the fabric of existence and manifestation?

Evi fished a tiny chemblade out of her morphcoat pocket and gestured it at him as she approached. The blade part was a sharp, hazy distortion in the air. "I remember those marks. You're Trow's culinarian." She barked a pained laugh. "I knew an assassin would be sent, but could they really do no better than *you*? You can gut a fish so you can kill a woman?"

"They didn't let me cook fish on Trow. Like they wouldn't let you deviate from your flight path."

"How many of you are there?"

"I'm one of a kind," he replied deadpan.

"*Assassins.* How did you even get here?"

Sentace couldn't read her expression, which was flattened by exhaustion. He'd have to tread more carefully than he had with

Molinar, especially as his relief at finding Evi felt dangerous, complacent. He needed her to hear him out, needed her cooperation and her wings, no matter how uncomfortable alliance and reliance felt.

"I'm resourceful," he answered. He didn't want to complicate things by bringing up his Trowan attendees, who had lacked the entire range of common sense and underestimated a massive, clandestine, multiversal organization.

Evi stepped forward to where the light hit her eyes. The iris color changed as the viewing angle shifted: Trowan eyes, like his. If she hadn't attacked him immediately, she would have noticed his eyes and they both might have ended up in better shape.

She looked down at him fiercely as if she could light him on fire by anger alone. It didn't match the handful of memories he had of her: quiet and soft, smarter than everyone in the room, gifting an occasional laugh that lit the whole crowd. Sentace knew a lot about Evi Omai, but she barely recognized him, probably only recalled the meals themselves, eaten at the back of the restaurant where he served unsanctioned foods. He'd snuck her liquor, another reason her memories might be fuzzy and his impression might be off.

Sentace led with honesty and mutual disdain. "I volunteered to hunt you so I could get the only free pass off Trow after they locked everything down post-fire. The administration wants you captured or killed. If I send back fake proof of your death, they'll put the matter to rest and let both of us go, free to start new lives while Trow finishes burning itself to the ground. If I don't, Trow will bend their own edicts and send *real* assassins, ones who know the multiverse and can track you down anywhere. You know the size of the bounty the government would be spiteful enough to put on your head."

Evi's tough facade cracked, lines creasing around her eyes as she winced. She knew Trow's spite all too well. Hardening back up, she said, "Free passes from Trow's iron grip don't mean anything out here."

She strode over, knelt on his chest, and readied the chemblade at his jugular. Something tied to her wrist like a bracelet caught Sentace's eye: the crystalline touchstone the Casthen had given each of the expendables they'd dropped off. If they were both on equal footing, that changed everything. As her hand came down with the chemblade, Sentace blurted the first lie he thought would stop her. "I know where it is."

Evi paused but didn't look surprised, didn't look like she believed him.

A sound snagged Sentace's focus away. He swiveled his head so his better ear faced the side of the ship. A low metallic groan, like power servos. Evi turned a beat later.

A two-meter-tall form rounded the corner of the ship and vaulted smoothly onto the ramp. A pistol glave was pointed at Evi. "Greetings, dearie," it said through a hollow, stilted vocal emitter. "How agreeable of you to bring a pair of wings."

Sentace recognized this competitor from the dropship. A small aquatic creature housed within the armored brainpan drove the mechanized humanoid skeleton and its synthetic musculature. The body's strange alloys and materials looked to have fared better in these environments than the augmented legs of the other fellow. A beefy spine formed the trunk, captured in a hard rib cage lattice. The muscled loaded on its frame looked to be for power but not flexibility. Raindrops made a strange pattering music across its many components.

Evi dismounted from Sentace's chest and placed herself in line with the cockpit, where she couldn't be fired upon without damaging the ship's controls. Sentace felt a burst of pride that he'd used this move too, back in the tower.

The creature said, "My moniker is Jito. You do not have to die, if you will behave."

"Oh," Evi exhaled, "I have done more than enough behaving for one life." With that, she stepped back and cued the bay-doors to close using her neural halo connection with the ship.

The big folds of metal irised inward. Sentace, on the ramp portion, was rolled outside. Jito made a mighty leap to get *inside*, but Sentace twisted to hook its feet with his. Their combined weight toppled them outside while the door shut.

"Don't leave!" Sentace bellowed at the closing folds, hoping Evi could hear. There were smarter things to say but they wouldn't fit in a couple words. Sentace landed on his belly, face against the fungus pad. The restraints on his wrists and ankles weren't as brittle as he'd hoped.

Jito levered upright to its feet with powered speed and pointed its glave at Sentace, only to be distracted by the ship's rumbling engines popping on. The vessel's belly tilted as it rose, which tore wounds in the fungal tissues it was wedged in. The blood that gushed out split into giant plumes of mist that the rain made even wider and more opaque.

Obscured, Sentace crawled to safety on the rock of the huge drainage shelf. It wasn't much safer, angling down to sea with a flash flood ripping across its surface, but solid rock felt good.

Jito was not as quick. Evi fired up the back jets, blasting Jito sideways. It rolled to a stop near Sentace. One shoulder, an arm, and a quarter of its rib cage were melting into lumps.

"She is not"—Jito's voice box cut in and out—"agreeeeeable any... more." It struggled to shove its torso up and tear away from the damaged half. The incandescent metal remains of the arm were left steaming and hissing in the rainfall.

"Trowans really aren't," Sentace concurred as he shimmied over to burn off his restraints on the hot metal.

Jito wobbled to its feet, muscular action glitching on one side. Steam ribboned from the jagged ends.

All damned, its remaining arm was the one holding the glave. Jito fired a volley of bright darts into the fungal sponge around Evi's ship. Thick clouds bloomed across her field of sight, stymieing the already cramped takeoff. Jito dashed into the cloud while grabbing something at its hip. Three loud *pop* sounds detonated before Sentace could react. Doors breached, slamming down. Then Evi screamed.

"Crimes," Sentace swore. Now was the time to flee... but he didn't come all this way, and have mercy collide him and Evi together, for one of these degenerates to kill her and take the ship and strand him again.

Jito's mech was tall enough to pinpoint through the rain and the blood-mist. Sentace sprinted and tackled it with his entire exhausted weight. Jito's glave rapid-fired mid-collision. Radiant darts sprayed the ship's ceiling, ruining a skylight. Sentace grappled Jito to the floor with sluggish movements, beyond spent. He wrested Jito's glave away and made the decision to slide it inside to Evi.

Hand empty, Jito overpowered Sentace's hold and slammed a palm around his throat. If the pain of the impact wasn't enough, he felt the clicks of a ratcheting tendon. Jito stood and lifted Sentace almost clear off the ground.

"Help," he mouthed at Evi.

She stood inside at a psychological crossroads, her face blank and the pistol glave half raised. She could leave them both. She didn't owe Sentace anything, not even for saving her.

His bruised windpipe compressed, face raging with pulsing, tingling heat. His vision muddied to match his hearing, the whooshing of constricted blood, the world disappearing.

Rap rap rap. Glave shots. Jito's legs buckled and its whole body tumbled, taking Sentace along by the throat. They slammed into the white water of a flash flood river carrying them toward the cliff and to ocean below.

Sentace flattened and sought traction, feeling all of Jito's weight hauling on his airway. He sputtered through buffeting waves. Screw Evi—he could only rely on himself. He grappled around Jito's body until his palm landed on a spare of the explosives it had used on the ship. He fumbled at the mechanism until it detonated. Concussive force plowed the water back around them, shorted Jito's electrical systems, and released its ratcheting tendon.

Sentace gasped air and clung to the rim of the flood channel. Jito's frame began to wash down the incline. A random instinct made Sentace grab Jito's brain case. It detached like an escape pod and let the rest of the body go, tumbling through rapids until it spilled over the cliff.

Drained, Sentace clawed and kicked out of the waterfall trough, back to solid stone. He draped there, skull against the cold, wet surface. He closed his eyes, gulped air, and let the chaos start to fade.

A distressed part of his brain listened for the sound of Evi's ship taking off. He had nothing left in him to get up or run or plead.

The rain moved on at last, giving way to the rushing sound of water vacating the mountainside. The sun bludgeoned its rays through the storm. Sentace was hungry. His weary mind went back to the marshes he'd seen at a distance and whether they had hibernating pellerwasps like back home. Dumplings sounded good. Or ramia.

Evi crouched by his head. She brandished the glave, ready to put a hole in his brain. With her other hand, she offered to help him up.

Sentace rolled supine and gazed up at her while clutching the fishbowl of a head to his chest. The creature inside, Jito, writhed orange and furious against the glassy walls.

She nodded at the thing. "How many others?"

Have you killed. Was that what she meant? The faces of the augmented man and Molinar flashed in his mind, the imagery mashed together like a nightmare. He replied, "Saved two. Killed two. Still a few hundred less than your flames." The jab was unnecessary, and bad, but it came out of him anyway.

Evi went quiet. She had no higher ground.

Was killing for self-defense acceptable? To protect another? To incite revolution? To free a people? Violence was a tool, Sentace had come to believe, like a knife or mallet or sieve. It had purpose. Use cases. Extreme ones, but it did.

The heat of action gave way to a cold rationality. The water and the chill stripped his thinking raw, absolving him of the last few days.

Evi asked, "Why did you save that?" Her edgy tone suggested she wanted to kill it.

Sentace held up the skull jar, droplets slithering down the pearly material and blurring the leggy little xenid inside. Delirium setting in, he didn't know how else to respond but laugh at the absurdity of having grabbed it in the first place. "It can't do anything now, can it? Might know or be worth something. No point throwing away opportunities."

Like me, he meant to imply. *Like Trow did.*

He craned his head all the way backward to get a glimpse of Evi Omai, hoping to see he'd gotten through her wall somehow.

His irises, from her angle, would have changed from brown to something like blue in the motion, reminding her that he came from the same home. The same stricture and poverty and rage.

She stared at him with a deep, blank look that was, perhaps, her signature or resting face... and he started to integrate, in a way that terrified him, how little he actually knew of this woman beyond the fiction he'd fashioned of her to justify his own ends.

- CASTHEN GAIN -

MIDDLE GROUND

E vi's damaged ship flew well enough to reach safer, lusher terrain where Sentace could source ingredients for a meal that he hoped would turn her friendlier.

Time had cracked open this gigantic architecture, forming bowl valleys invaded by sunshine. Sentace wandered from the main dome to adjoining chambers where ancient trees, like hunched giants, had bullied through the industrial shell. Plants flourished, forming luminous oases in the murk. The floods had topped up ponds and streams, and animals of all sort congregated in the rain-refreshed spaces. Bassy frog calls resonated while glassy cicadas clicked out of sync. These alive places calmed Sentace's anxiety, but he kept the ship in sight, expecting Evi to take off once she finished repairs. He worried that the knife she'd given him was a mercy gift, to not abandon him unarmed. Even if she stayed, other competitors would be coming for the ship, likely more of a target now than any fake "anomaly." Certainly more visible.

Sentace hurried, knee-deep in flooded rock channels that tree roots had wrenched open. Water chestnuts, perlcress herb... each discovery added to a dish forming in his mind. He'd need all his skills to soften someone as wary and hardened as Evi Omai.

Swift as phantoms, a school of pale bodies darted out of rock recesses. Mouths spread and a horrific number of legs wriggled as they swarmed his hands and legs. He yelped and on reflex both jumped back and grabbed one of the creatures. Pain needled across his skin, chased by an electrifying frizz of neurotoxin. He boosted up to dry land and kicked the other long bodies off his ankles.

Sentace lifted what looked like an eel or olm—an aquatic salamander—but with centipede-style legs. The floods must have washed them out from underground passages. It was blind and slimy—easily brained on a rock—and after a sniff and some probing, Sentace deemed it edible. He hung the eel-thing off his laden satchel beside a game bird then glanced at the shiny black ship again, like a nervous tic. Evi crawled on the vessel's spine and filled cracks in the moonroof.

In the next chamber, grasslike structures vibrated in a blurry carpet, smooth and powder blue, spotted with flowering reddish ground cover and marshy divots. Sentace spied reeds that had fibrous balls attached. He made an elated noise and lowered his ear to one. No buzzing—fantastic. A load went into the satchel.

One final treasure on the way back: cones fallen from a stiff plant stalk twice his height and growing from the ceiling. Sentace found a universe that cracked the pithy scales and exposed fatty, squishy nuts inside. He was transported back to his childhood days wandering through nature; taking plants apart, digging in the earth and upending rocks, peeling bark, shaking trees. It was part of the reason he hadn't ended up like the other Trowan kids: he had been parented by nature, while they only had the strictures of society and school. When his mother fell sick from overwork at the grindstone of Trowan perfectionism, then from one of the many diseases that genetic homogeny incubated, he couldn't rely on her to take care of him, and he couldn't rely on the Trowan system to take care of *her*. So he managed both. Young Sentace broke the demarcation rules and ventured into the wilderness for the food and medicine his mother needed to survive.

What had Evi's childhood been like? What had broken her in the best way?

Back in the crumbled, stadium-sized dome, Evi was pasting organic sealant on hull gouges. The vessel sat parked in a meadow, with streams winding around it to a drainage in the middle. Glowing organisms turned the water molten burgundy-orange and made the dome feel like the inside of a candle. Hopefully the cozy mood would help file down Evi's edges.

She greeted Sentace by readying Jito's pistol glave. Like a hero at the end of a legend, she looked weary and trial-battered and weather-beaten, with wet hair sticking to her skin and blood drying like battle paint across her face. Maybe she was too damaged to ever soften up. Many had seen her arson as an act of insanity.

As he neared, he noticed more of her slow blinks and deep sighs. Her skin was cracked and her hair dull. This poor arsonist needed nourishment. Looking over the starship, which was not her Trowan vessel but a custom patchwork of expensive and budget parts, he wondered if she had poured everything of herself into affording it, after leaving home. Rather, in order to build a *new* home.

Evi side-eyed him while moving on to some welding. Sentace pretended to ignore her and dropped his haul near a small universe in the meadow. First order: build a fire and a support structure for a pot. The labor grew tougher as he ran on final fumes of energy.

Evi had let him use a medical spray on his clipped ear and singed head, but his face felt tight with bruises, one cheek swelled, his throat was tender, his shoulder muscles might've torn, and his hip might've fractured, among other bodily protests. Maybe he was just getting old.

Sentace chewed on a few caffeine-packed leaves while he planned two preparations of the salamander eel thing. After shearing off its hideous abundance of legs, he blanched it to more easily scrape away the slimy surface parts then filleted half to marinate. The other half he cut thirty times through all its thousand tiny bones to avoid the task of removing them. He filled the universe with fragrant wood chip smoke and staked the skewered filets upright inside.

Evi passed by and missed a step, blinking at the universe full of whorling grey. Her morphcoat's feather layer bristled in response to her startled mood. "You made it… into a smoker?"

He gave her a little smile.

Evi's barrier broke with a tiny laugh that she turned around to hide.

Alright—winning her over might be possible. Sentace boiled a restorative tea of elm bark and flowering herbs. He peeled the fibrous cocoons he'd collected down to the plump, dormant pellerwasp curled inside each. The hard iridescent exoskeleton he discarded, then fried the protein-rich morsels in hot seed oil from Evi's supplies. The cocoons were a delicacy made of saliva, like some bird nests were, except these became creamy and cheese-like once simmered.

A sharp *slap* drew Sentace's attention from the pan: Evi, patting her starship's side. She kept glancing over as pleasant aromas wafted her way—the opposite version of his paranoia that she'd leave.

Finally she strode over. Held out at arm's length was the container with the xenid called Jito. "I'm not keeping this. It could escape."

Sentace *willed* his brain to switch from cooking to speaking and not wonder what the creature tasted like boiled in its own shell. He guessed Jito was a nareid species, a semi-corporeal. Through the milkiness of the skull housing, he couldn't tell if Jito was suspended in liquid or if the translucent movement was an extension of its frilly, leggy, fire-colored body. It looked pissed, whirling and attacking the sides when Sentace took the container.

Resisting the urge to place it near the fire to see what happened, he said, "Jito seemed pretty polite, earlier. What if it's harmless? Or useful?"

"What if it's a parasite?"

It did look like one. However...

"Is it a necessary death?" Sentace asked softly. He thought of Chiidi and how individuals could end up in situations like this Casthen experiment merely by getting caught in the riptide of multiversal factions. He didn't want to believe that this was another world that made murderers of good people.

Evi's expression pinched, and she went quiet for a long while before turning away, saying, "The ship has a toxic cargo chamber. It can go in there. For now."

Anything open-ended with her felt good; a door that hadn't been slammed.

Sentace left his own judgment open-ended, too, and with a chuckle he set Jito's container on a rock opposite his fire, like a guest. There was a chance it could read lips or comprehend sound vibrations without an aural system, so he said, "Didn't you mention something about behaving? Behave and I'll try to keep her from chucking you. Maybe think about your life choices and all that."

There was the possibility that this Jito was some sort of kingpin, like Molinar, and saving its life might earn them a reward. Besides all that, Sentace felt a newfound hesitation at immediately casting away hinderances. For once that looked the same as throwing out something potentially valuable.

Even Chiidi. He needed Evi compliant in order to go back for them.

Sentace lifted a basket of drenched cone nuts into the nearby universe after clearing out the smoke. Hydrogen behaved as he'd hoped: the structure of the nuts transformed, distending with internal moisture bubbles. He removed them and compressed the liquid out, giving the nuts a spongy, grain-like texture. They went into the broth with the chopped eel, liver, seasonings, and creamy cocoons. With quick motions Sentace rocked the pan, folding the mixture over itself in smooth waves. Meanwhile he watched Evi stomping back and forth in the bay, rearranging bins. She crisscrossed a painted section of floor that had glyphs reading WI90NN-1238.

Raising his voice to cross the way, Sentace asked, "Does your ship have a name?"

"No." A new kind of silence stretched, then she added, "I'm still getting to know it."

Sentace wanted to ask what her own crash course into the multiverse had been. Like him, she would have been experiencing new wonders for the first time, trying to navigate her own ignorance of dangerous multicultural dynamics, while trying to stay clandestine, away from the resources that could make things easier, like Cartographer help.

He saved those questions—they were third meal topics. Instead he asked, "Does your ship have a scour?" A bright feeling rose in him at the thought of a scour's deep clean. The multi-species technology not only washed skin, hair, and clothes, and took care of elimination, but it could heal some superficial injuries and bruising. Sentace needed all of those things.

"No." Then that pause again, as if information was a currency and she calculated what to give him, what to buy. "I'll install one in the lower deck. Someday."

Evi cocked her head at him and seemed to notice something new. She rifled around in a wall compartment and threw him a bundle of garments. Unlike his, these were dry. Sentace unfolded an overcoat with three blast holes in it, and split skirt trousers with a scorch line up one side. "They didn't have a good time, did they," Sentace commented.

Evi stifled a laugh as she came to sit by the fire. "Excuse you. I'm a *great* time." Her morphcoat diminished into a silky black mesh in response to the heat.

Sentace changed clothes, then fished a small cloth out of his things, dipped it in hot water, and offered it to Evi. "Face."

She sniffed it pointedly, as if he might've tried to poison her, and he couldn't tell if she was being sarcastic. She washed the blood and grease away, then let her wet hair down and attempted to detangle it. The ends were asymmetric where she'd cut it in a statement of protest. Steam billowed around her as the wet strands fell into the fire. Sweat glistened over her golden skin. She really did look like a legend in the flesh: the firestarter, Evi Omai. The insane arsonist of Trow. The tired, beleaguered woman who just wanted to be free.

Sentace filtered the tea. It smelled and tasted sweet, and would aid digestion and calm the mind. He floated one of the blossoms on the surface.

Evi scrutinized the meal operation with a look that could be real or mocking, and Sentace felt off-footed that he couldn't interpret her expressions or humor yet, how to tell if her toughness was a facade. She said, "Not bad, chef. Fine dining at the ass-end of the multiverse's worst planet."

"Cheers." He handed her a mug, which she didn't take. Sentace took a sip. "If I wanted to poison you, I wouldn't go through this much effort."

"True," she drawled. "It was easy to poison that Trowan administrator, before the subsidiary work mandate could pass. I don't think anyone else realized it was you."

Maybe Sentace was right to not let his guard down yet. Evi was wittier and sharper than he'd expected.

She accepted the tea. "My ship doesn't have an autopilot system yet."

"Noted."

"Thank you for your service, by the way." Evi took a long, slow sip.

Oh, for the poisoning. His heart did a little flip. Hadn't he meant to thank her first? To pay respect to something that felt daring and legendary... to protect it from retaliation...

Sentace assembled his gratitude in the finishing touches of his dishes. Water chestnuts added texture to the creamy nut-grain dish, plus a sprinkling of perlcress herb—not just vitamins and minerals, but a tangy, peppery flavor for brightness among the rich eel and cheesy sauce. He topped the dish with the smoked eel and the fried wasps tossed with sliced lime leaves. The wasps' abdomens were another creamy, meaty flavor while the remaining hard shell added a burnt tang that would complement the smokiness of the softer eel. For garnish: leftover marinade passed through the small universe transformed it into savory-sweet red threads. On top he balanced seasoned vegetable peels that dried into crisp, oniony curls in the universe's edge. Last, a bloody splash of crimson sauce around the rim of the serving plate, to acknowledge their shared origin.

This absolutely was not a Trowan dish, which made him proud.

With it he finished two side dishes: minced bird meat and vegetables breaded in some of Evi's ration bits, then fried in bite-sized pieces, and a simple salad of greens and shavings of a vine-fruit that had a seedy melon texture, crunchy and slightly bitter.

While he zoned out wondering how to pickle it, Evi took her plate and a first bite. She made an involuntary moan of pleasure. Her eyes widened and she slowed her chewing, savoring the flavors. She tried the sauce and other elements in combinations, then concluded, "Now I remember why multiversal travelers came from far and wide for your dishes."

Some color was returning to her cheeks, and a tenderness softened her eyes as she experienced care for the time since leaving home, from what Sentace could judge.

He tried a bite, mostly pleased. A hind part of his brain was already making revisions to the recipe.

Evi crunched on a wasp and wiped juices from her lips. The Casthen's crystalline touchstone tied on her wrist glowed as they said it would when the anomaly was in proximity. Sentace's pulse skipped a beat and he jerked upright, but as Evi lowered her arm, the firelight reflection left it.

He stared. "I guessed you sought asylum with the Casthen, but why do you have one of those? Don't tell me they decided you weren't valuable enough to take under their wing?"

"Guess not." A wisp of pain wrinkled Evi's face then was gone. She ate a few bites of salad distractedly, calculating what to divulge. "I gave the Casthen our planet. I told them where it was and what I had done to upend the Trowan government, the planet basically free for the taking. It's special, after all, with so many universes." She waved sarcastically at the universe beside them right now and two others far overhead. "I was given this test: find the anomaly, and they would take me in."

Sentace scoffed, "How could you have trusted in systems, in institutions, in communities, after Trow? The Casthen are as evil as they come."

"The *Casthen*"—Evi raised her voice—"are a home for the unappreciated, the cast-offs. They elevate potential. They offer purpose. *That's* why I came to them. They're a place for people like us."

"They expect you to die out here. The anomaly isn't real, and that"—he nodded at the touchstone—"is to track *us*, if it's not just a pointless trinket."

"If there's no anomaly," Evi argued, "they would have simply executed your group and the ones that came before it. They would have executed me and taken my ship for parts."

Sentace had to admit he didn't know what other point there would be, especially since their physical labor or the meat of their bodies had to be more useful in any number of the Casthen's other operations. "Testing grounds, maybe, like we're live game and they'll release some kind of weapon on us."

Evi rolled her eyes, the iris color shifting through copper, then purple, then indigo as the viewing angle changed. "Listen to you trying to justify your closed-mindedness. The Casthen Foremaster gave me a map of the zones they've already searched, as well as a guess at the proximity where the touchstone reacts, and that they aren't sure if it's on the move or stationary."

Even if Sentace was wrong, it still seemed impossible to find this energy anomaly in over half a planet of uninhabited space.

Even with a ship, the search would take weeks. Sentace kept his mouth shut this time.

Evi scraped her plate clean of sauce using one of the fried bird poppers. "I believe the Foremaster who recruited me will keep her word. You can either join me, or stay here, because I'm not flying you to headquarters, and I'm not flying into the exosphere to be shot down. No one who comes to the Casthen's homeworld leaves to tell about it unless they themselves are Casthen. The only way out is through."

Sentace quested, "And if you find the anomaly, and the Casthen take it and kill you anyway?"

"You sure like to speculate on things that are very damned uncertain. I can't control that outcome. I have to trust, like I trusted myself when I set fire to the forests and fields. I keep moving forward."

Evi Omai, the firebrand, set adrift from their world to light up new ones. Or was she an ember, a guttering flame about to burn out, hoping for a breath to revive her? She cuddled into her morphcoat, which fluffed to feathers as temperatures dropped while their fire guttered out too. The softer light revealed a weary, vulnerable woman underneath the fantasy that Sentace had built up in his mind. Evi wasn't an indestructible revolutionary who had all the answers and the valor to act on them.

She kept moving forward, but he wondered if she looked back enough—if trauma would even let her look over her shoulder, just yet. Sentace's old rage flared as he thought of the collateral— the flora and fauna and citizens lost, the things he'd mourned and couldn't bring himself to think of as a necessary cost... not until he could also see the future that it had bought.

Evi stood and headed into the ship.

When she paused and looked back at him pointedly, he asked,

"This means I can stay?"

"I haven't shot you or closed the door, have I? You can be a bit dense, it seems."

"I'm cautious. This is your space."

"How considerate."

"When required."

She shook her head and continued inside, waving him over. "I said you could join my search or stay here. Up to you."

There was only one answer. Sentace grabbed his supplies and Jito, who he'd nearly forgotten about entirely.

Evi closed the bay-doors behind them. When Sentace gave the seams a doubtful look, she said, "I put up more safeguards, and we're only going to get three hours of sleep. Put it in there." She indicated a toxic containment cabinet on the wall.

Sentace stuck Jito inside and stopped himself from muttering an apology. If the xenid needed food or another resource to live, there was no way to ask.

Closed up, the ship was hushed and dark, with a handful of sleepy lights in the cockpit and a couple of dim spotlights in the bay. He followed Evi down the ramp to the lower deck and a perpendicular hallway. A door straight ahead led to the engine room. Blank walls on either side were perfect spots for the scour installation Evi wanted. On each end of the hall were identical bedrooms.

The sight of a sophisticated place to rest cracked his exhaustion open in a new way. He was definitely entering the giddy, second wind stage of sleep deprivation. Sentace pitched his hands on his hips. "Two beds, huh."

Evi smacked the back of his head. "On the right, Sentace Ketch."

She headed left. Before the door closed, he glimpsed cozy lights and glass things and sprays of color that looked like plants.

A nest of personality in this sterile ship.

"Evi," he began, stopping her in the doorway. His jest might have gone against the grain of the tone between them, slipping out as fatigue loosened his grip on his thoughts. When Evi turned, he couldn't figure out how to phrase the reassurance he wanted to give her that his intentions were safe, despite his joke. This alliance might not even last long enough to label. "You're obviously smart, badass, and hot beyond any rating system possible, but my reasons for chasing after you were platonic. I admired your audacity. To meet you is enough."

"Yeah... I know." She frowned, looking a little flustered. "Get some sleep, Sentace."

Clicking his tongue at himself, he turned to survey his room: a simple bed with a fluffy bedspread, a single pillow, and nothing else. For now, it was luxury. He shed his borrowed clothes, slid under the covers, tried then failed to find a less injured side of his body to lay on, and plummeted deep into sleep anyway.

10

DEEP DIVE

A few hours of sleep on a comfy bed in pitch black silence had been divine. Refreshed, Sentace could handle the fact that Evi barely had any plan for what to do next in the search for the anomaly.

He'd held breakfast hostage until she granted him a favor and flew to where he'd abandoned Chiidi. He semi-lied by omission, telling her there was something important he'd left along with a food cache. The latter was true unless the iredimi had eaten everything. Sentace figured it was better not to ask Evi if he could add another passenger, and instead let her fall for the little guy herself.

Chiidi was still damp and lethargic, but had seemed awed first that Sentace had returned, and second at being able to meet the infamous Evi Omai. They had poured on the charm and adoration, eyes huge and glistening, and gained Evi's reluctant blessing to come along.

Sentace opened a container in the ship's bay. "This heated

dry-bin is for cargo that—"

"Like Chiidi!" they squeaked and clambered inside the insulated shell. It didn't seem like they'd fit, but most of that volume was fur, which compressed against the perforated walls and started to blow dry.

"Yep." Sentace chuckled. "Stay cuddled in here, and be quiet, and Boss Evi might keep you around."

"Get it. Am dead weight. Need lay low."

"Good stuff." Sentace patted the lid and closed it gently.

The ship cruised at low altitude. Evi sat in the cockpit running tests on how long their gloss-derivative fuel would last. The Casthen must have supplied her with that expensive fuel source. The creatures whose brains it came from were all extinct, he'd thought.

Evi was quieter and more calculated than the firecracker Sentace had expected. Ignoring him entirely, she crunched numbers and doodled complicated course plots, adjusting for curvature, finding geometry that would make the most of their resources. Sentace meanwhile plotted the space in the refrigerated cargo compartment, not counting on Evi factoring food resupply into her chart. At least he'd managed to invert a heat harvester unit to function as an indoor stove.

He finished slicing the vegetables that wouldn't last another day. Evi had her geometries and he had his: curls, sticks, cubes, mince. He bundled the colorful textures and a cold sauce into wraps of leaf membrane, making bite-sized packages of flavor. Vegetable pierced the top in petal shapes with herb leaves. He delivered the plate to Evi in the cockpit. That big brain needed fuel.

Evi took a piece absently, but the first bite pulled all her focus to the plate. "How do you do that? It's like a painting."

He flicked a finger through her holosplays full of math. "Just as impressive."

Evi grumbled and ate another wrap. "But much less rewarding."

The touchstone on her wrist glistened when she moved, but it still hadn't glowed during any of their travel looping the desert of the planet's tidal lock. Sentace wondered if the anomaly lay deeper than the touchstone's response range, but kept that notion to himself.

After a final bite of food, Evi wiped her hands on her trousers and slipped her fingers into the pliable substrate of the twitch drive pads on the console. With a muscular motion too slight for Sentace to see, she veered the ship and kicked up the velocity.

He asked, "Where did you buy this ship? I haven't seen its style."

"Because it's not any style. I stripped my Trowan carrier down to her bones and sold everything else. Then I bought new parts, a slimmer profile, gutted, built out the lower level... bounced between markets getting more modifications piecemeal, doing jobs, exchanges, running from pursuit, building my getaway as I was getting away. It's a mix of organic and inorganic, rare and common. It's not done being remade, like me."

Sentace finally found a topic she would ramble about.

"It's small," he noted, "but built for at least two. Way too cramped for five or six. Did you anticipate a crew?"

"I didn't say you could stay for good, Sentace Ketch."

"You didn't say I couldn't."

She shook her head but her lips were soft, hiding a smile.

"You went after everything you wanted," he observed. "Right away. The ship, the gear, the Casthen."

The neural halo hovering around her head was a new sort, too. It required an implant in the brain but linked the pilot's senses to a ship as if the vessel were a second form wrapping around theirs, with capabilities far beyond the door-opening and UI navigation of her previous kind. Sentace tapped the edge of that thin ring of light.

Evi flopped her head back at him. "That's impolite."

"Sorry."

"What else was I going to do but go after everything? I gave myself the freedom to become someone new. Why wait to get there?"

Why wait.

What was Sentace becoming? Edges were peeking through as he shed old habits and values from his past, but he couldn't see his new shape yet. Maybe Evi didn't know what she was becoming either, and was just moving, moving, moving—unafraid of moving blind, or unable to stop even if she wanted. "You're overpowered," Sentace muttered.

He thought he noticed color blush into her cheeks. He swooped the plate up and took it over to the hot box.

"Chi."

The top cracked open and a spindly pink hand slipped out to grab a couple pieces. Happy noises were muffled by the lid.

Sentace ate the rest while unlocking the cabinet that held Jito, just to check that the xenid was still alive. It squirmed in its transparent housing, tendrils pulsing. Was its color greyer than before?

After tidying up, he resigned himself to being bored once again. Boredom on a climate-controlled ship, away from danger, with good company, and a bed... he would take it over excitement on the ground. To pass the time, he did some heavy lifting, because although he was thick-set and strong, the past days had shown him that his physical strength and endurance still wasn't enough. He also couldn't rely on Evi or the ship being around for long.

They flew for days, low enough to periodically fall into danger from hidden megafauna and avian flocks and carnivorous alien flora. They skirted around evidence of the dropped prisoners making their own search efforts: part of a facility activated to rotate it and allow access inside… a reservoir's dam blown to bits, draining it for exploration… and a frenetic three-way battle that broke out around the mouth of ancient catacombs.

The ship gave Sentace and Evi an advantage over the others, but there was still a chance someone else could find the anomaly first —especially if it was deep, deep down—or kill all the competition, or whatever other win-state the Casthen were orchestrating. Sentace bundled his agitation up along with the opinion that all of them were stupid to even try, and he shoved that out of his concern for now.

The sun never set or rose, the light changing only as Evi flew to different sides of the twilight belt. Sentace lost track of time except to count by hunger, by meals. Evi counted by fuel percentage dropping and uncharted zones shrinking.

The touchstone never glowed. Sentace puffed up because it proved his theory right, but it also made him morose because this endeavor felt pointless and Evi's devotion to it became more dogged the more that hope dried up… which explained a lot about her.

They concluded that the anomaly was nowhere near the bright side of the planet, so Evi flew through the habitable twilight band toward the dark.

The daylessness stretched on so long, Chiidi had finally dried.

The restlessness simmering in Sentace churned up dark, intrusive thoughts.

Jito's pistol glave rested on the cargo. The chemblade, too. He had a stash of poisonous herbs. He'd built up a degree of trust with Evi—he could break it. He could argue about this being futile and her too stubborn to see it, or modify the zone information to show even less area left to cover, or force her to fly where he wanted at glavepoint.

He could take control of this situation.

Evi landed the ship atop a thin tower of wreckage where they had a total view of the landscape they'd covered. Sentace was once again impressed by her skill as a pilot, able to land on the tiniest island, in the narrowest canyon, or upon the foot's-breadth ridge of a mountain.

The engines cut off. Evi's loud sigh pressed into the silence. Her morphcoat bristled into black scales standing on end.

Ghosted across the cockpit window were the lines Evi had flown, arcing all across the view. Unless the anomaly was on the move, it seemed impossible that they would have missed it anywhere.

Sentace felt the weight of Evi's heart dropping. He swallowed his arguments, his I-told-you-so, and his own frustration. Instead of pushing her to a snapping point, he stamped down his dark thoughts and he ground up some dried lion's tooth root with warm spices, and brewed them in nut milk and burnt sugar to make a creamy, soothing beverage.

She took the mug from him and cradled it between her palms, dropping her face to inhale before sighing again. Her halo glowed eerie rays through the cloud of steam. "I hear you."

Sentace drank while peering past the overlay to the landscape beyond. Dark rainforests carpeted the laps of craggy mountains. Craters pitted it so deep and numerous they became an ocean. More ancient megastructure lay sunken below. Stars dusted across the sea's smooth kilometers, and across the horizon to the sky, and up through the cracked skylight overhead, surrounding them.

"Evi…"

"Just let me think."

"*Evi.*" Sentace stared at the faint edges of architecture beneath the sea. They hadn't flown over an entrance. "Your ship doesn't have guns?"

She snorted. "You have no idea what those cost."

What ship *didn't* have guns? Anyway, it would be hard to blow a way inside.

He scanned for universes near the structure. "C-Center class. This ship's aquatic too, eh?"

Evi frowned at him, then took a thoughtful slurp of her drink and followed his gaze to the ocean. "Crimes, I'm so tired."

Sentace felt that in his soul.

He opened his mouth to spout something encouraging, but Evi straightened and said, "Let's go. You figure out a way to break inside."

She cruised the ship slow around the visible parts of the submerged structure. Sentace felt immediate relief at having a puzzle to work on. He was also glad for his love of water and swimming, because it took several dives to check his arms' indicators on various universes that bisected the architecture. Then, a few stops on land to fetch ingredients and refresh all their supplies. He fashioned a small payload from tree gum, toad secretions, plant sap, and various components collected in the ship.

Dropped into the proper universe, it did... nothing.

He tweaked his recipe, placated Evi with snacks, and tried again. The explosion happened at the rind, not the universe interior —too soon and too strong. "Happens sometimes," he murmured, humor heading into the gutter because there were only ingredients for one more try.

He did another dive to double check his indicators and recalculate parameters, then built the last bomb, sacrificing some of his spice chemicals for a new coating.

This payload detonated like an underwater sunrise and took out the entire rotted ceiling.

"Bravo." Evi smirked and brought the ship to a hover. "Got

there eventually."

"Thank you for your patience during this trying time."

A laugh cracked Evi open, and it was good to feel the tension defuse all the way.

Sobering up, Sentace ventured, "Can we agree that if there's no touchstone response in this ocean, we accept that the anomaly is a lie and chart a course for the Casthen facility?"

Evi made another of her delayed answers by descending the ship through the sea's surface tension. It transformed to an aquatic configuration with a rush of sound like a metallic icefall, and a pressure change that sent prickles across Sentace's skin. It felt as if the water membrane was a universe rind, and the ship translated itself to pass through.

"Agreed," Evi conceded quietly. "I'm going to turn on the scalar gravity but it gets spotty, so… hold on or strap in."

Sentace decided to hold on.

Evi tipped the ship nose-down, flicked on the fore lights, and proceeded to cruise deeper. The scalar gravity initiated, immensely unsettling: a soundless pressure buffet all around, then a sense of compression. Dimples of space tugged him in a grid-like pattern of interference waves, as if a hundred uncoordinated hands were trying to steady him all at once. His inner ear grew so confused he was glad he'd skipped a meal, otherwise it would have come up again. The shooting pains returned like laser fire bouncing between the walls of his skull.

"First time?" Evi asked, on their joke still.

"Please shut up."

Translucent walls encompassed them as they descended. The size of the drowned structure dizzied him further. The atmospheric light seen through the ship's moonroof was swallowed by the fathoms, dunking them in a void where luminescent fish drifted like blurry candles.

Evi brought an orientation reticle across the cockpit windows: the only thing keeping Sentace grounded as he lost sense of how deep they'd gone. He wasn't up in the air, but the immensity or the sense of free fall from the wonky scalar gravity flipped his fear of heights into a dread of depths.

Despite his heart trying to escape his chest, this was a beautiful sight. The ship's beams fractured across the bones of civilization, the deteriorating ceilings and walls channeling the light into dreamy, shifting geometries. Oceanic flora thrived: extravagant varieties of coral, grassy algal species, red and pink anemone with tentacles longer than Evi's hair. Forests of rooted kelp struggled to gather light, their strands of tattered lace and pearly bulbs stretching thirty meters long before they tangled in the remains of the roof.

Evi piloted carefully, seeking passages large enough to fit the ship through. Bioluminescence replaced starlight in the darkness. Gradually, the hard mineral architecture gave way, as if it had been clothing something beneath.

"Is this…" Sentace trailed off while Evi widened the fore light into a full, soft glow around them. He couldn't name these surfaces… some were porous but plump, as if filled with invisible matter, and others were smooth and undulating like layered veils. Materials shifted with the viewing angle, like his and Evi's eyes, and some crystalline walls he could barely make out without the cockpit's guidance overlay.

Evi prodded him. "Is this…?"

"Do you think… Is this Graven architecture?"

"I've never seen anything Graven, except the stellar egresses."

"Me neither." But it looked unexplainable enough. Ethereal enough. Like stepping into a different dimension, sensing a thing displaced from another time… that's how objects from the Graven era had been described to him by patrons. The Graven had created the multiverse, somehow, fracturing laws of existence to break one universe apart into so many.

Evi said, "This planet feels like it's been rewritten multiple times. Constructs built, abandoned, repurposed, shelled over. I wonder if… perhaps that revision process went on all the way to Graven eras?"

Sentace had heard that said of other places in the multiverse as well. The bones of Graven architecture had been colonized with new civilizations and modern materials.

Deeper in, they encountered universe bubbles. Big ones. Evi slowed at each until the rind edge passed barely into the cockpit. Flux licked the nose of the ship, watering the view, stressing the world into a new language. Sentace stuck his arms in to assess his indicator sleeves and decide how safe it was for them and the ship before she flew farther in. The answer was often no, in part because Evi's ship was such a medley of unusual parts. If they ever escaped this planet, he would have to sit her down and consult on what to change to expand the ship's crossover potential.

"The universes here…" Sentace started. "It's been bothering me. They feel intentional in a way they didn't back home." It was time to stop thinking of Trow as home. Evi was building home around her, with this ship. Sentace didn't know what home looked like for him yet—he'd always wanted to make a name for himself in the culinary scene across the multiverse, always imagined being itinerant, going where was novel or where he was needed. Maybe he didn't require a new home at all.

"That's an eerie thought," Evi replied. "No technology or process can *make* universes."

"Not since the Graven were alive."

Evi visibly shuddered. Her brow knit as she concentrated on navigating a labyrinth of narrow channels and vestibules, some intact and others broken. Many passages had only inches of room to spare, and though Sentace trusted Evi's skill, it was hard to watch.

He was glad he'd opted to not wake Chiidi earlier. They didn't need an aquaphobic iredimi freaking out at being kilometers deep in the sea.

Sentace asked, "Your Casthen Foremaster didn't say what the anomaly was? They have no clue?"

"Didn't say. The energy is faint. Maybe not even a thing, maybe just an error somewhere, a system online that shouldn't be. A piece of technology that won't die."

That was what Molinar had speculated. A weapon. She'd sounded certain of it. Everyone else had suspected some Casthen machination requiring human players: a test or a game.

Evi's tone flattened when she added, "If it was something special... you'd think they would have spared no expense to investigate."

Sentace stayed silent, thrilled that Evi was coming around to his side on her own. They'd flown all the way into this watery tomb for some pretty sightseeing, but at least they were safe.

Evi, of course, doubled down on her flight path. After a passage of white-knuckle narrowness, Sentace felt the ship bob to a surface, pressures shedding off the hull, scalar gravity dissolving. This huge chamber had a dry upper half like an upended glass. The walls and ceiling were made of cells of bubbled gel-like material. Universes impinged on it, changing the color and luminosity of the sea water within each.

Evi reversed the ship to a ring of dry floor around the circumference of the undersea dome. With a catch of distress, she said,

"I can't make out any route past this. We'll go back. There were a few paths I could try instead."

"Evi," Sentace whispered, voice cracking on the second syllable. He cradled her wrist and turned it twice, making sure it wasn't just reflections this time. The touchstone had a glow of its own.

Evi cautiously levered up from the pilot's seat, staring. She didn't pull her arm away, as if his hand anchored the truth of what she was seeing, as if it might have been a trick of the light or their exhaustion. Her chest swelled with air, joy filling her up so much he imagined she'd rise on tiptoes. In a grand exhale, she said, "I knew it."

Sentace finally realized: this discovery was something that was *hers*, like her freedom and her ship. This search was something she was doing for her own agency.

She pulled her wrist away and pored through the limited scans available. "There's still no opening we fit through."

Sentace kept the joke to himself. "We walk." He peered out the front view. "This place looks designed for beings about our size."

"It's underwater." She didn't add "idiot," but there was a tone.

It was indeed underwater. There didn't look to be dry passages other than the ring, and there were no cloudsuits on the ship for underwater travel. Given a new puzzle, Sentace's mind sped up. "I saw a lizard once."

"Sentace, *please*."

"Bear with me. I have an idea."

COLD GRAVE

t took a few hours for Sentace to sort the components he had on hand, backtrack to areas of different sea life for new materials, seek out universes in between to alter substances, and to sift through the technology on the ship... altogether an unhinged recipe that Evi had no confidence in by the end, but Sentace was energized to try.

Almost manic with fatigue, he plastered his makeshift rebreather over his head, shed down to his undergarments, and stepped off of the dry ring of the underwater chamber, into the water. He gave Evi a wink that she rolled her eyes at, then submerged.

The rebreather was a hydrophobic skin made from kelp membrane and fish secretions, which allowed air to stick and form a bubble that inflated and deflated with his breaths. Paired with micronized algae and the components of a broken cloudsuit, it would keep their oxygen situation stable unless they crossed into a universe where one of the elements failed.

"It's perfect." High on his own genius, Sentace tested the

tension with a big exhale.

Evi finished piling her hair up in magnetic webbing, then fiddled with the fit of the collar. Her morphcoat changed to a waterproof material and became skin-tight over her muscles and curves. "You're deranged."

"I know. Get in here."

Sentace swam a few test dives and located a passage out of the chamber. The rebreather film clung to his head, then peeled away, before slicking back down again in a bizarre, clammy sensation accompanied by fizzing sounds.

"I hate this," Evi declared after testing hers.

"Yeah, well. It's not too late to head up and alert the Casthen that we found their anomaly. Let this become their problem."

She shook her head. "The touchstone doesn't work as a flare beacon until it's completely registered at closer proximity, in case the anomaly is something that moves, apparently. Besides, I want to know what this thing is before the Casthen hear about it."

Did she have the guts to try to hold it hostage? Sentace laughed, which fluttered the rebreather bubble in a worrisome way.

Evi took the lead, the touchstone on her wrist growing brighter or dimmer as it resonated with the energy signature they sought. They swam downward through canyon-like passages arranged in rows similar to a beehive. The material, however, was nothing Sentace recognized, resembling mineralized plumes of vapor. Gigantic dead coral? The walls grew self-luminous and less opaque, revealing the architecture at large. This water felt moonlit, and became warmer until it reached that equalized temperature where the border between skin and sea seemed to disappear. Sentace was unlikely to ever experience an environment like this again in his lifetime. Even if they found nothing, it was a worthwhile swim.

As the quantity of universes increased, Sentace moved into

the lead to find safe routes. Most bubbles were the size of rooms, and stuck together at the edges like a giant foam. The smaller the universes became, the more densely they packed against one another, and a chilling realization dawned on Sentace.

"Why did you stop?" Evi asked.

"We're nearing the center of a universe cluster that started kilometers back. Those edge bubbles were just too large to register that they were part of *this*. I've never seen anything like it."

"Old Graven technology gone haywire?"

"Mercy's tits," Sentace swore, "that would be worth a fortune."

"Language," Evi chastised, but her shoulders shook with a giggle.

Nothing in here looked like technology. It felt organic and otherworldly, like they were swimming into a vast body that had been buried, petrified, drowned. The commingled blue, purple, and pearly white candescence felt funereal.

Their progress slowed dramatically to navigate not only the labyrinth of universes, but a convolution of valleys, columns, combs, and spires.

Sentace grazed his arm into another rind, watching the lines of a wing on his wrist turn gold and warn that this universe would slowly dissolve human skin. The next: dots prickled hot over his knuckles, and blue flickered through the ink swirls around his forearm. Their oxygen would fail in there. The seawater in a larger neighboring universe agitated into myriad spots of sonoluminescence, micro explosions—he didn't need indicators to see it meant death.

The next passageway opened to a grand chamber, the far walls of which Sentace could barely make out. Filling the inside were universes of increasingly smaller volume, all stuck together in a puzzled geometry of potentially deadly spaces. At their core was an area a few meters across that glowed so thickly with an ethereal light, folding and unfolding to the rhythm of a bass pulsation, that Sentace's mind couldn't make sense of it. He thought of a plasma core or some alien battery.

He tugged Evi to his side where they still had room to tread water.

"It's there," she said, hushed with reverence.

Sentace flicked the brilliant touchstone on her wrist. A burst of rays cut the water. "We're probably close enough to consider this thing charged. We could go back."

"I think it would uncharge if we left. And…" Evi gazed at the cluster of universes and that gossamer light that seemed to peel back dimensions to something soft and raw beneath reality. "I need to make sure… that this is something the Casthen should even *have*."

Sentace hadn't considered that the anomaly might be something to destroy or protect rather than hand over. He was oddly proud of her for thinking so wide-scale, but he wasn't about to throw away their ticket to freedom. Anyway, the hard decisions could wait. Sentace squared himself before this maze of progressively? smaller universes. Tight squeezes; literally no room for error. It would be impossible to stop swimming without sinking through another rind or crossing a limb over accidentally. He'd have very little time to judge safety by look, feel, and indications.

He said, "Follow behind me, not too close, and memorize the route as best you can. If you see me bail, backtrack immediately. There's no guarantee that central universe will be kind to us."

Evi's throat bobbed with a nervous swallow. "I suppose… you're likely the only person in the multiverse who could get through this."

"So the competition stood no chance from the start, huh?" He flashed her a smile, smothered his fear with confidence, and took off.

Sentace streamlined his body to fit the first universe, one meter across. Scales and inked petals changed tone on his arm, and a deep itch cropped around subcutaneous beads of metal as they liquefied. Not too bad. Most universes weren't instantaneous death or violent transformation, they were subtle physics adjustments that would destroy you over time.

The color in the universe ahead was off, the wavelengths over-bent. He dived straight down instead, this universe heating his body and turning the rebreather film stodgy. A few seconds was safe.

Left, the toxin lines on his skin spelled danger when he skimmed the rind.

He chose right. Ahead. Up.

His sweating forehead mugged his oxygen up and made the collar fit wiggly. Blips of seawater leaked in. He tapped into reserves of calm, imagined himself cooking, where he regularly had ten things to pay attention to all at once.

The universe spaces grew tighter, squashed out of spherical shape by their connections to neighbors. Sentace kicked to orient sideways. His foot grazed a nearby rind into corrosive physics. In seconds, a strip of skin flayed off the top. The pieces sizzled into particles. Sentace choked back a scream, almost biting his tongue. Blood effervesced off his foot then coagulated in long strings. As he flailed to stay level, he caught a glimpse of Evi wide-eyed with terror behind him.

He had to keep going. A flesh wound—who cared. He clenched his teeth and swam through the rind of the next safest universe, where his skin paled all over, his heart skipped beats, and the wound grew pleasantly numb.

Up, up, left, through a tiny bubble bordered by death, and then gliding down. Infuriatingly, the central universe of the cluster felt less than five meters away at all times, but impossible to head straight toward. The path was disorienting, divisions everywhere, walls of hazy flux where universal laws changed, where languages shifted… the broken space felt like some godly being had taken a fist to the window of the world and shattered it, cracks radiating from the impact.

Sentace wriggled deeper into universes barely his body's width. Like an eel caught by the head, he twisted frantically as he struggled to both swim and use his arms to test translations. His shoulders brushed rinds on either side, blistering on the left and bruising on the right.

Finally, the center.

He pulled his hands in front to touch the rind, a billowing, half-meter thick wall of pearlescent light. The translation flux passed over his knuckles, wrist, forearms. The indicators fired and colored and morphed in a combination he hadn't seen before, but was, theoretically, safe. Too far in to care anymore, and sinking anyway, he flutter-kicked the rest of his body inside and unfurled in the new space of the central universe, several meters across at last.

"Damn, Evi, we ma—" A horrible muffled noise cut him off. Twisting around, he collided with Evi curling into him, clutching her head. The relief in his chest tightened into a knot as he caught her shoulders.

"What is it?" he yelled.

Evi's rebreather film was taut and vibrating with her scream, starting to froth as if it might fail. On her next inhale, when the bubble clung over her face, Sentace gently folded his palm over her mouth. Her gaze anchored to his and she got the message, swallowed her shriek, breathed through her nose, and stilled her thrash to a trembling. He watched as her eyes dulled and wrinkles of pain striped her forehead.

Something had happened during her crossover into this

universe. The damage to her skin and clothing was no worse than his, the result of too many rapid conversions. Internal, then. He asked, "Do you need to leave this universe?"

Evi tried to shake her head no, but winced and fought off more squirming. Some injury in her head, perhaps.

"Take a moment." He laid his palms on her temples with slight pressure. She shut her eyes.

They could float without treading water in here. The gravity dimpled toward the center, similar to the universe that had cushioned Sentace's tower fall, but far weaker. Light permeated from nowhere and everywhere, soft and white with a hint of alpenglow. When Evi opened her eyes and looked around, her gaze was softer, her irises shifting between lavender and green with the angle.

"Evi?"

She fell to his chest when he let go of her. Voice husky, she explained, "My new neural implant... middle of the brain. For the halo. Cheap work."

Sentace felt a stab of responsibility at misjudging her safety, forgetting to ask what material her modification was so he could factor that into his calculations.

Evi noticed his expression, and pushed away. "I'll be alright, for now. It isn't active outside of the ship's proximity."

She did not look very "alright for now." Sentace realized she was one of those people who toughed things out rather than being honest or asking for help. Maybe they did belong together.

Her head swiveled, taking in the universe bubble they'd reached. This one was a near-perfect sphere due to the sheer number and tiny sizes of the universes bubbling off its sides. A shadowy object levitated in the nucleus. "What *is* it?"

Sentace peered up for his first good look.

Through billows of watery light, he made out a lump of black material the size of his torso. The edges were rough or ashen. It looked to be mineral… unless those lines were wood grain? Layers? Beneath a smoky metallic sheen, the object's translucency revealed deeper textures and flaws inside. Like decayed, petrified wood that was also volcanic glass.

Evi whispered, "Is this lightseep obsidian?"

She said that as if lightseep was deadly. Was it? Sentace's pulse jumped. "Lightseep can't be moved in space, it's dimensional matter. But this does look… Crimes, who knows."

"We haven't tried moving it yet."

Despite how dead this weird hunk of material looked, it did possess a mesmerizing aura. It was raw and primal, swaddled in dimensions Sentace couldn't fathom with human senses. His skin prickled, the feeling of a thousand eyes watching him. All his fears getting into this universe paled in comparison to the idea of touching this thing, as if he'd be obliterated, metamorphosed, or transported on contact.

"It looks decayed," Evi said with a hint of melancholy. "Long dead."

Braver than him, she reached to it. Invisible standing waves purled around her fingers. The radiance of the touchstone refracted off the ripples. It looked like a slow-moving music: ruffling then smooth, singing then echoing.

Sentace said, "Looks inert, but clearly it's emitting enough energy or spacetime distortion or whatever to have been picked up by the Casthen's instruments. This is either the anomaly, or this point *in space* is." He glanced over all the indicators on his arms again. "I don't understand how it's so *bright* in here."

"What if there are harmful rays we can't see?" Evi said. "We might be as good as dead already."

"The busted implant makes you extra cheery."

She patted his cheek as she swam upward. "Hold my ankle while I reach."

Sentace grabbed her foot as it swooshed past his head. Her momentum pulled them both to the universe center. Sentace back-stroked while letting his arm stretch to drift Evi in range of the material, both her arms extended in a cradling motion. His heart hammered away, sweat in his eyes and a bitter taste on his tongue.

Evi's fingertips touched down on the object.

Nothing happened. She didn't turn to dust or fold into another plane of existence. The matter didn't wake up like dormant technology. The architecture around them didn't collapse, and the object moved when she drew it into her arms, so it wasn't the Graven's lightseep obsidian.

For a moment, Sentace settled back on the idea that the universe itself was emitting the anomalous energy, and this chunk of matter they were fixating on was simply the remains of some poor thing that had wandered in. Evi's deadly ray idea didn't seem so far-fetched.

Sentace tugged her down. "Let's get it back to the ship. I'm worried about the rebreathers failing. And about lethal light—thanks for that one."

"What if one of these universes destroys it?"

They would be re-navigating the labyrinth of universe foam, although this time it would start hard and get easier as the bubbles grew in volume. Sentace said, "I have no idea what this material is, so we'll have to take the chance."

He took the anomaly from her and found it strangely spongy. When he pressed his arm against its side, very few indicators responded. He could tell it was biological, or had been at one point.

Sentace held it close and a little in front as he swam to

the border universe they'd entered by. Admittedly, he hadn't memorized the route—too long. He pushed the anomaly through rinds, feeling like he was steering an asteroid out in space. His gaze stayed glued to the thing's edge to monitor any change each universe's physics inflicted, but bizarrely, the conversions appeared more like the universe reacted *to the anomaly*, not the other way around.

He fought back chills and focused on his course. A few accidents later—nothing worse than the seared foot or Evi's busted implant—they were back inside vast universes and big chambers, and the anomaly was no worse for having crossed over thirty or more times.

"Your touchstone is still bright," Sentace observed. "This is it."

Assembling all the conversion reactions and universe specs in his head, Sentace had the feeling that in the right sequence of environments, this dead matter might be rejuvenated. He contemplated this during the swim back to the ship. Once they surfaced and Sentace rested the anomaly on dry ground—it didn't react to atmosphere—he said, "Evi, I think this is *meat*."

She tore off her rebreather and gaped at him. "How do you... Well, I guess if anyone knows about meat, it's you."

"I think it's *Graven* meat."

"Now that, deranged chef, is too far. The Graven lived eons ago. No corpses remain."

"Maybe something with a lot of Graven genetics, then?" The slight sponginess, the muscle fiber texture, the mineral veins that looked like bones...

"Sentace Ketch. You and I, grown up on a closed-off planet, have never seen anything Graven, even rendered in art. How are you so sure?"

"I've seen different types of matter, and crossovers, and

universe types. I've served countless species of xenid with unique physiology. I understand the physical world like a scientist would, even though I don't have the words for things. This anomaly's material is unlike anything I've interacted with before. If that's not the definition of Graven, I'm not sure what is."

The Graven civilization—believed by some to have generated the multiverse—had died out but left a great deal of their architecture, their lightseep obsidian cities, and their technology. Not all of it was understood, but it was immensely powerful, valuable, and impossible to recreate by any modern means.

Evi poked a finger at the dark tissues. "Let's say you aren't wrong. This could be worth fortunes. The big factions would kill for it. The Casthen have killed for it already with numerous groups like yours."

Sentace didn't have an argument, except: "I don't know what the factions would do with it, but it doesn't feel like something the Casthen should have." His investigations had uncovered countless grisly stories about the biological experiments the Casthen were known for.

"No," Evi agreed, her volume dropping as defeat took over. "*Meat*. All damned, Sentace."

"So we don't activate the beacon. Agreed?"

"Agreed. Get on land, clear our heads, then discuss." She walked to the ship while signaling the bay-doors to open using her neural link. The doors obliged, but Evi *screamed*. Her wrecked implant...

Sentace charged over and made to help her to her feet, but she stopped him with a hand. "Evi, this is bad."

"Just... pain. The commands."

"Can you disable it?"

"No," she exhaled. Her jaw set. "I'll just handle it. I can turn some systems off. Feels like a corkscrew turning..."

Sentace scowled at her. He carried the anomaly into the ship, finding that its weight didn't match its volume, didn't feel like carrying a body. He set it to one side of the bay and turned a spotlight on.

Evi changed to dry clothes and let her hair down. Her morphcoat transformed from rubbery waterproof to a woolen textile, but some of its dark color glitched where Evi had been holding the anomaly. An energetic stain? The floor beneath the anomaly looked strangely shadowed as well. Both of them and now the ship, marked with this thing's essence.

"Do you think you can pilot us out of here?" No answer. "Evi?"

She was levering down into the pilot's seat while her face pinched in agony. The cockpit burst to life with holosplays that her fingers flicked through, adjusting the neural link and powering off assists. She gradually slumped in relief, but her skin had paled and dewed, and exhaustion dulled her eyes.

She rolled her head to look at the anomaly. "None of this is what I expected."

Beneath the ocean, entombed in ancient architecture, in a web of universe bubbles, a worn-down relic of decay with no apparent purpose. Sentace hadn't expected the anomaly to be real at all, so he'd had no expectations to break. What had Evi hoped to find?

Freedom. That's what they both ultimately wanted. A freedom that meant not watching your every action as well as your back; not beholden to a code, not living beneath a heel.

Sentace settled against the ship wall and let his brain empty and his body decompress.

He would not have managed all of this alone. For once, allowing someone else in his space hadn't dragged him down. He'd been rigid about self-reliance to avoid being restricted by others, but he was hobbling himself with his own beliefs, keeping alive the Trowan way he'd been so desperate to escape. This was another piece he could shed.

GAME OVER

Evi was not alright.

The ocean was straightforward piloting, but once back in the air with the ship converted to planetary flight, Evi had too much input and not enough editing, as she described it.

"Land there." Sentace pointed to a flat sea cliff plateau.

Errors harassed her in the wraparound holosplay, red warnings and miscalibrations spreading like a rash. Little seizures. Blips. She'd turned too many auxiliary systems offline. Sentace had to carefully prod her hands in the twitch drive more than once to keep the ship from rolling.

"Evi Omai. *Land.*"

She made a pained, stubborn whimper, but complied.

The ship touched down with an uncharacteristic clunk. Evi fell unconscious the moment the engines shut off. Her nose smacked the console again and started bleeding.

"Crimes' sake." Sentace propped her up and wiped her face. The neural halo thread fell slack around her neck.

She needed sleep and nutrition. Sentace did too after swimming for at least an hour in deadly spaces, plus the mental stress of recovering a relic that could either get him killed or pay fortunes.

He dug around in their remaining food stores. Chiidi had been at it! The little rascal.

The meadow outside didn't promise much, but Sentace was good at making something from nothing. He'd glimpsed animal herds of some kind… maybe meat could be back on the menu.

First he fetched a blanket to toss over Evi. The climate control was offline, and couldn't tell she was chilled. Her morphcoat had fluffed up into down feathers and fleecy mesh.

Sentace grabbed a satchel, opened the bay-doors, and strode out with new purpose. A rabbit bolted from underfoot and across the meadow. He'd look for snare material later. Jito's pistol glave was somewhere, but he didn't understand its ammunition. Too bad he didn't have a hawk.

He entered a big universe several meters away and sunken into the ground, which converted to volcanic sand. The air felt snappy and full of static. Sentace's skin heated while the coil of lilies beneath his elbow turned from chalky to coal—bad sign. He exited and scouted nearby ravines, finding springs and plant life. He focused on foraging the micronutrients and herbs that would help Evi recover. Nutrition was medicine.

He rubbed what looked like a relative of wisterweed on a section of inked forearm that responded to histamine, and was pleased at the response. When he'd implemented the indicators as a way to catalog universe physics—a weird idea that Trow had disapproved of—he'd never imagined he might be on a new planet and need to test other foreign objects, too. These recent days, however harrowing, had validated the breadth of his skillset. Beneath his outward confidence, he'd been afraid that the parts of him that had developed on Trow would only be applicable *there* within that meticulously curated system.

Sentace headed back with enough ingredients for a light meal. Silhouetted by twilight, Evi's starship looked misshapen, unfinished, and perched in the hostile stance of some creature with too many wings. Its back opening cut the rays of the interior lights into spiked intersections. Three smaller beams bobbed like errant stars in the murk, approaching the ship and growing brighter.

"*Shit.*" He'd forgotten all about the competition and had let old rhythms distract him. There was no sign of Evi awake inside. Sentace sprinted. Pain shot up his burned foot and his injured hip. He invited a new rhythm. Pain. Focus. Bloodlust.

Sounds of a struggle preceded him: a stifled yell, scuffling, gurgling, and something high-pitched like a scream stretched thin.

The lights were touchstones. At least three people were fighting one another... for not just the ship but the *anomaly*, the entire prize packaged up for the taking.

Glave fire striped the air. Not an energy type, but metallic, whistling into the sky as it missed. A childlike figure fired on a gigantic one. Sentace recognized the chketin silhouette: a humanoid of immense size, bloated with muscle and covered in armor-like skin. A meat mallet fist slammed down on the girl, who crumpled.

The chketin pivoted to barrel at the third figure. Sentace, very weaponless, crouched and arced over to the fallen human. She was a dead tangle of skin-and-bone limbs and long, pale hair. Her drug-flushed skin was turning purple. Sentace prized the glave out of her hand, thrilled to see that it indicated its ammo on the side. Five shots of whatever this was.

Between him and the ship's tail, the other two fought. The chketin had no weapon except his size, which was enough, but his coordination was sluggish. Malnutrition, perhaps. Lightheaded. Good.

The chketin flailed, punching air, careening at nothing. His opponent was too backlit to make out except that it was an unfamiliar xenid: a bony, skinless quadruped whose torso raised up from a squat abdomen, topped with an elongated, dish-shaped head.

Neither had spotted Sentace yet. He was shaking, exhausted, muzzy. He raised his stolen glave pistol at the chketin and strode forward, but was swarmed by more attackers from both sides. A blade silvered through the dark. An explosive flash razed in front of him.

Sentace ducked, but no strike or blast came. Battle sounds rioted through the ringing in his ears. A figure charged him from behind. He fired at their forehead but they kept rushing. He tackled low and swept through nothing, only to hit the ground.

Dizziness took the reins of his nervous system. Ahead, through his visual noise, a crowd poured into the ship and blotted out the light. Sentace shouted Evi's name before his mind registered the wrongness of what he was seeing. His yell drew the chketin's attention.

This wasn't real.

The chketin loomed half again Sentace's size in every dimension. His body was all purple-grey skin shredded in scar patterns. No neck, just muscle, with a round, pockmarked head perched atop and missing an eye, as if *any* chketin needed to look more like they'd been through a grinder.

The giant charged. Sentace leaped sideways in time to only take a glancing blow to his hip. *Oh*—that was absolutely real. Pain crashed through his pelvis while he spun torso-first into the dirt. He rolled while the chketin's fist cratered the ground. On his back, he fired two glave shots that *barely* buried into the chketin's hide.

The behemoth's attention wrenched away suddenly. He fought empty air beside himself then roared and strode past Sentace, toward the ship.

Confused, Sentace rolled to all fours and got a better look at the other xenid, the quadruped. It resembled a deep sea creature dragged into the air, decompressed and mineralized. Its skull had a distorted jaw, like bone jowls, with two round nostrils, no eyes. Crustacean bastard. Its elongated forehead was like a dish perforated in chevron rows. An olfactory organ?

Hallucinations. It wasn't receiving, it was *emitting*. Sentace groaned. Just what his mushy brain needed. An enemy that could make you see illusions.

As he rose, the view blurred into dreamy fragments of fallacy. His senses smeared between this and that, pasting over real things with fake, and fake corroding into real. It was like a flip book of universe conversions, a constant translation, destruction, and formation.

Several meters ahead, the chketin toppled. Sentace hadn't seen from *what*, and his simmering fears turned to a boil.

The crustacean xenid opened its beak to reveal three mouths' worth of terrifyingly human-looking teeth. A shriek tore across them. Ship metal and landscape rock resonated at the same frequency of that horrific vibration. Cracks and snaps pinged all around as things broke. More than a few of those things were the chketin's bones. He didn't get up again.

The crustacean crawled up the ship ramp. Finlike appendages with webbed fingers moved it silently except for the click of claw tips. The touchstone hanging around its torso blazed in proximity to the anomaly until the rays flashed: confirmation level. The xenid crushed the touchstone to activate its beacon mode. The rays converged and a cord of brilliance shot skyward. Thunder cracked and reverberated outward in stages while aurorae flooded in its wake. Some long range signal or pinged satellite or higher atmosphere spark was now letting the Casthen know the anomaly had been found.

Sentace whimpered a swear. There was no coming back from this.

Two shots left. He staggered up the ramp, aiming at the crustacean's forehead plate. His vision filled with phantom attackers blurring together, a nightmare mash-up of punches and teeth and weaponry. Sentace was a creature of instinct with hair-trigger anxiety: he couldn't help flinching and re-aiming. The faces and bodies mobbed him, the roof collapsed, everything was underwater again, then falling... endless falling. Acrophobia hijacked him, starting to buckle him into the ground.

Sentace roared and fired the moment *something* felt right. One—miss. Two—this hit, and the crustacean emitted another sharp, nauseating screech. Ten migraines punched Sentace in the face. Through it, a familiar sound reached him. *Chiidi's shriek.* Sentace's focus whipped together. Chiidi was clinging protectively over unconscious Evi's seat.

The attacker rushed the pair with its mouth open like a mower. Chiidi's gangly arms flailed out and caught its jaw at top and bottom, holding it back even as they toppled onto Evi's lap. She awoke with a start, her eyes wide as she saw the looming being. She kicked its mouth *hard* while bundling Chiidi against her chest. Then the hallucinations hit. Quaking uncontrollably, Evi clutched her head and screamed like she had when the implant was damaged. Her ship responded. Systems slammed online all at once. Lights blazed. Locks opened. The engine howled.

The crab bastard reeled backward, overwhelmed. Seizing the

chance, Sentace body slammed it sideways, crushing it forehead-first against the wall's—surprise—now opened toxic containment locker. Vials of something foul broke inside, and the brainpan that contained Jito smashed on the floor, releasing the creature in a frenzy of writhing tentacles.

Sentace muscled the attacker's beak shut and tried to shove its head into the acid spill. He felt vibrations build. Hallucinations mapped over the indicators under his skin. Morphing stories of warning and trauma played out there in signs his nervous system was conditioned to obey. His focus slipped, letting more illusions burgeon in his mind, filling the ship with Trowan wildfire that convinced his skin of heat and his lungs of smoke. Out of the flames, a very real bony appendage plowed into his cheek.

Starbursts crazed through the static of Sentace's visual field. Everything slowed while a howl consumed his auditory world. Three zipping sounds pierced through—the third accompanied a sizzling tear across his gut. Shallow, just into the fat.

Evi was firing a pistol glaive from the cockpit. Firing at what real or illusory thing, who knew. Sentace threw himself to the floor. Trowan corpses littered the bay. He grasped at phantom objects—various weapons, knives, foodstuffs—until one was real: the fist-sized heat harvester he'd inverted into a stove. Better than nothing.

Abruptly, the hallucinations shut off. Objects, sounds, and sensations winked out of existence.

In the stark emptiness, a feral whistling reverberated inside the ship. The crab bastard screamed as... Sentace blinked to make sure he was seeing true. The creature Jito, broken out of its container, was squirming into the orifices of the attacker's skull.

Tendrils slithered into perforations, plugged emitters, invaded nostrils, and cracked teeth as it burrowed its mass through the mouth.

Sentace yelped a swear and backed away from the horrific sight.

No, this was a chance to finish things. This final effort could take everything he had left. Ignoring Jito's invasion, he wrestled the crustacean xenid onto its back and reached through its awful abundance of legs to shove the heat harvester into a seam of bony plates, then stomped until the object lodged inside the abdomen.

The creature's scream blotted Sentace's vision into another grey hash. By feel alone he hooked his arms around its rear appendages and—wringing out his last strength, roaring until his voice broke—he dragged it down the ramp, across the meadow, and into the universe nearby.

The rind slicked over Sentace's body. Sweat boiled into steam and left a rime of salt over his skin. His panting breaths felt like fire. He hauled the bastard all the way inside before dropping it and stumbling out. The heat harvester turned white hot in these physics. The monster was steamed in its own carapace. Pallid flesh plumped and bulged, cracking through shell.

Jito wriggled out of the innards of the brain case and crawled pathetically across the dirt and the universe rind.

The crustacean's wailing faded into the quiet wheeze of its last moisture evaporating. The fumes made it through the rind, carrying a stench like fermented scallops left baking in the sun.

Sentace would not be making seafood again for a long time.

He fell onto his back, let his quivering limbs go slack, and gazed up at the touchstone-turned-beacon hanging like a star. "Game over."

13

TWO FUTURES

"Oh. You aren't dead," Evi declared. Her voice was raw. Sentace had passed out where he lay after the fight. He wasn't sure whether to be offended or charmed by her flat tone. "I'm a lucky guy."

"Just extremely tough." Evi bent over him, haloed by the beacon in the sky. Brown hair cascaded over her shoulder and tickled his face.

"How is your…" He tapped his temple.

"Bad. But I'm tough, too."

Sentace rolled his aching head to one side to confirm the wreckage of the attacker's body on the other side of the rind. The heating element was a melted lump in the center of bulging tissues and shell shards.

Just outside of the rind, Jito twitched in a floppy heap. Chiidi approached it.

Parasite.

"Chi! Watch ou—" Sentace shot to a sitting position, which

smacked his head straight into Evi's.

She reeled back, hissing a string of swears, then kicked him hard on his bruised hip. He doubled back over.

Chiidi picked Jito up by one ribbony limb and squeaked, "A scholm! They canno get in iredimi head. Too small. Pea brain." Chiidi's wide mouth opened in a grin as they waved Jito like a wet flag.

Evi stifled a laugh. "Find a new jar or something for it, will you?"

"Yes, boss!" Chiidi bounded back to the ship with Jito flapping in their grip.

Sentace said, "*Now* you're letting it live?"

"What if it was invading that xenid to save us?"

"What if it was trying to get a new body, to kill us?"

Evi offered a hand down to help him up. "I wonder if we'll agree on something, someday."

Sentace groaned with stiffness and bruises as he accepted her help. He jabbed a thumb skyward. "We agreed not to set a beacon off."

It reflected as a perfect ring around her irises when she gazed up. "Right. So much for keeping the anomaly a secret. What do we do?"

"We get… farther away from here. Hidden from the Casthen until they arrive." More than that, the chketin's and the girl's corpses were ripening, mingling with the crabby stench into a thoroughly unappetizing setting. "And then we eat."

"Starving."

Sentace held his breath and hobbled to the chketin, who had no useful possessions, and sported the Casthen insignia branded on one meaty shoulder. Next, the addict girl, who was carrying a number of high-end medical supplies. Better, Sentace realized the hallucinations had affected animals as well: a dead rabbit, some vole-type mammals, and several fallen songbirds littered the meadow. He took the rabbit and joined Evi at the ship.

"Thank you," she said quietly as he limped by.

"I'm keeping track of how many times I save your life."

She clapped him on the back and left her warm palm lingering. "Unluckily for you, I have low self-preservation. My life isn't worth much to me."

She said it so matter-of-fact, like it was a piece of her she'd turned around and around until it became smooth and dull. Sentace fell silent as he mulled over this sad new facet of Evi Omai. Another scar from Trow. Was this why she'd lit those fires—with nothing to lose?

Sentace said, "I'll have to stick around and save it enough times then." He *did* need her dead, actually. Fake dead, to get the Trowan government to call his mission a success and stop pursuing her, then cut him loose. He made a mental note to ask her to play dead for him later, when the mood was better.

Inside the ship bay, Chiidi had shoved Jito into a jar of medical solution. The scholm resembled a frilly, jeweled, emaciated squid. Though desaturated, the iridophores in its skin reflected tiny metallic flashes in a respiratory rhythm, indicating it was still alive. Sentace decided to be glad, because they needed more things to be glad about right now.

He herded Chiidi back into hiding, just in case the Casthen arrived early. Evi took the pilfered painkillers and adjusted the ship's systems so she could fly carefully into the volcanic hinterland. There the shadow of a large outcrop provided ample cover.

Evi trudged to the medical supplies and folded herself wearily onto the floor to investigate exactly how cheap her implant was and how to compensate.

Sentace had already patched up, so he applied himself to sorting out a meal again, something grounding but not too heavy. He still wasn't sure whether to serve Evi fine dining or homespun meals. She was fine enough for fine, but the times she'd visited the back of his restaurant had been to enjoy a break from the perfectionist Trowan norms. Maybe there was a middle ground. Homey, but elevated.

"Just make it delicious," he muttered as he headed out to start a primitive fire. Wild, open flame was comforting after a career of mostly high-tech heating surfaces and tools. The simplicity and tactility made his brain work in a refreshed way.

While hunting for swelterstones, he noticed the ship jets had cracked open local geology, including several geodes. The largest one became Sentace's makeshift oven. He plopped in some salt-rising bread dough he'd improvised from Evi's ground ration blocks, then closed the split and nestled it on a bed of embers.

He butchered the rabbit and lightly pan fried its saddle before wrapping it in the wisterweed lookalike and another meat he'd been aging that came apart in papery sheets. He fried the bundle in oil.

"That smells incredible," Evi said, lured over. She had washed up and tied her hair so it fell in loops. As she sat by the fire, her morphcoat grew wispy over her banded top.

Sentace handed her a flute of digestive tea cut with citrus blossom liquor and rock sugar. He nodded at the neural halo laying slack around her neck. "No luck?"

"I think I figured out how to tell the ship to ignore it. The hybrid systems I chose are… problematic now."

"Is fleeing before the Casthen arrive even an option?"

"I could manage. It's still a good ship." Evi swirled the flute, thinking. Sugar clinked against the glass. "But there is, still, nowhere to flee *to*. We're deep in the Casthen's palm and won't escape this solar system's universe without their fingers closing around us."

Sentace looked to the stars and couldn't see the enveloping rind from here, but there was something strangely prismatic about the exosphere. A force field?

Not one constellation or galaxy was familiar. Gazing spaceward felt like a new kind of free fall. He was immensely small, in the end, beneath this incomprehensibly massive and multidimensional world.

When he looked back down, the fire reflected in Evi's stare. An ember popped. She said, "Even if we managed to make it far away from here, the moment anyone realizes we have an object worth fortunes, we'll be the biggest bounty in the multiverse."

Sentace voiced the rest: "We wouldn't stand a chance."

That word kept feeling different, like it was changing temperature. *We.*

As tough as they were together, they were still naive and unequipped to take on all the multiversal factions and free operators at once. A Graven object was not a simple thing to fence. Like the immensity of the view above, this was too big for them to handle.

Sentace finished plating a salad of red and green bicolor crispa leaves packed with vitamins, mild but minty, plus a herb relative of ginger with bright floral notes. Delicate seaweed fronds for crunch and pop. Thin-shaved water shoots, hard and sweet. Wild pea curls. The greens stood upright like a miniature forest. Every bite would be different, ten courses in one. At the base pooled a sweet and acidic fermented sauce. He garnished the top with a swirl of gossamer flower stamens that glistened with nectar, and a sprinkling of savory luminescent grains.

"If we can't escape," Sentace said, "why not destroy the

anomaly? Torch it with the ship jets? Drop it in that volcano farther north? The acid river?"

Evi admired her plate, picked up a glowing bead of garnish, and flicked it into the fire. With a sizzle it burned away. "Then we have nothing to barter with. If we're empty handed, there's no reason for the Casthen to keep us alive."

"There's no reason either way. They've stripped us of the power to barter."

"But *we* aren't without value as long as we don't make ourselves their enemies." Evi swallowed a bite of salad and squeaked with pleasure. "All damned, are these weeds? Bravo, chef. See—your skills and imagination are unique, worth something. I have yet to see anyone do what you do with universes and rinds. The Casthen would find a use for you, *if* you have the opportunity to convince them so. Destroying or hiding the anomaly would ruin any chance of that."

Sentace let himself be warmed by the compliment and her enjoyment of the meal. He untangled his more complicated thoughts in silence while he sliced the wrapped rabbit into medallions—perfectly juicy in the center and fried crisp on the outside—garnished in an array of crimson arrowleaves. He dribbled a sauce into the pooling meat oils, together perfect for dipping the bread, which emerged from the geode oven in a quartz geometry. The outer crust's glaze had turned a metallic orange sheen.

Thinking back to the dropship... the Casthen soldier hadn't been dishonest about the competition. Cruel and flippant, sure. But the anomaly had been real, the touchstones had worked, and they'd given the prisoners a probability of success. There was a chance the Casthen would honor the prize of freedom, too.

"You're saying that if the Casthen don't let anyone but personnel exit this world, then the only way to survive—the only 'freedom' we can have—is to join their establishment? Evi, don't you realize how much that sounds like walking right back into the life of servitude we ran away from? The life you set fire to."

"I know... I chose to come here because they could protect me from Trow's retaliation. From assassins." She gestured at him ironically. "And I believed—still believe—that they could offer purpose and support to strays like us."

Her voice grew raspy as she turned a vulnerable side toward him. He didn't pursue the accusation. It was *him* stuck in old patterns again, balking at anything that bore resemblance to the hurts he'd sustained on Trow.

Sentace savored the rabbit, herb, and aged meat wraps while the fire guttered to coals and the knot of heaviness in his chest took on a name.

"The real dilemma," he said softly, finding his way, "is: should we survive by delivering this relic to the Casthen and letting them do unspeakable things with it? Do we hand power to the most morally condemnable faction in the multiverse? Or do we commit to our own destruction, but destroy the anomaly first, and save the future."

Evi stalled, sopping up the juices on her plate with bread, making the streaks even and straight. "I'm not a good enough person to make the right decision. There's too much uncertainty about what the anomaly actually is or could do or become. If something heinous results out of this choice in the future, can you live with that?"

"What if... something miraculous comes of it instead?" A waver crept into his voice. A shift inside him let walls down all at once, and new, lightweight thoughts floated in. "Isn't it just as possible that the correct choice is to let the Casthen develop this thing? It might revolutionize the multiverse in ways we can't fathom, which even the Casthen can't corrupt."

Evi caught his gaze and saw something that made her shoulders relax. "Crimes, you have reassuring arguments. Will you keep those up if I keep you around?"

"I thought you were keeping me around for the food." He smiled. Maybe this was simpler than they were making it out to be. Maybe there was only one choice.

They both had escaped Trowan oppression. The trauma of Sentace's old life had taught him how to play along, how to shoulder open room for agency where there was none, and how to keep his true values hidden but preserved. Instead of completely shunning community, establishment, and partnership, he should have realized how he'd grown able to function and stay tall despite it. They could maneuver through the Casthen order, too, and that didn't have to mean subscribing to the Casthen ethos.

He said, "If there is no right decision, and it's lose-lose, let's be as selfish as possible."

"What?"

"Let's choose to live. We're not heroes. You set a world on fire for a chance to thrive. I lied to and abandoned that same world for the same chance. We fled without looking back. Maybe we belong here."

Evi chuckled. "Are we villains if not heroes? Maybe citing a headcount would impress the Casthen."

"You would look far too impressive." Sentace's attention was itched by a distant sound. He tilted his head until it grew clear: a harsh tone washing over the valleys. Aircraft.

"Our judgment arrives," he announced. "Let's uh… keep Chiidi and Jito out of it."

"Obviously."

"And let's keep the cluster of universes to ourselves. If they ask, the anomaly was deep in the megastructure." Something felt personal about the place they'd found—not personal to him, but… he couldn't begin to explain. Hallowed. A tomb of universes: a grave marker etched into the fabric of the cosmos. A place that shouldn't be disturbed again.

Evi stood and looked worriedly in the direction of the incoming ships. Five of them, studded in lights, peeling out of the night. "This is a lot of secrets, Sentace. *No one* keeps secrets from the Casthen. I don't know why or how, or know much about their leader Çydanza, but it… it's just not done."

They were up against something too vast, they were out of time, and barely had a plan. If neither of them could think up an approach on the way, they would have to adapt as the situation unfolded.

Evi concluded, "This would be like that labyrinth of universes where any wrong move gets us killed, as simple as asking the wrong question or encountering the wrong person."

Sentace flashed her a winning smile. "And we got through that labyrinth, twice. So who better than us to attempt to keep a few secrets from the Casthen."

Evi deflated in mock surrender and shook her head. "You're deranged."

"You love it."

"It's growing on me."

VERDICTS

F lanked by warships, targeted by facility weaponry, and harassed by multiple spotlights, Evi piloted her ship to a landing pad nestled in the Casthen's main megastructure. Four soldiers had accompanied them inside to keep eyes on the anomaly. They were various species or hybrids, all obscured in dark uniforms covered with mismatched armor and blue metallic-glass masks. Sentace was sweating and jumpy with the fear that Chiidi wouldn't be able to stay quiet in their box. The Casthen seemed to relish his unease as a sign of their intimidation working rather than a secret under wraps.

Once the ship settled and the landing gear was locked, Evi opened the bay-doors to a surge of designer oxygen. The four soldiers and a team from outside wasted no time fetching a lift for the anomaly. A sinking feeling overtook Sentace as he watched the precious thing get hoisted out of his and Evi's control, out of their space, and into the vastness of Casthen operations. He was reminded of ants swarming in to carry away a drop of sugar as throngs of scientists descended upon the anomaly. It was ushered into a clear-walled quarantine room where the sheer number of curious personnel mobbed it out of sight.

Sentace had to remain at peace with this decision. Breathe.

He huddled in the cockpit with Evi. She whispered, "Let me do the talking. You're bad at it and just a prisoner, but I came here with prospects."

"You wound me." He clutched his chest. She was right though.

Evi settled her neural halo around her head and winced as the thread levitated.

"Evi."

"I want to remotely close and lock the ship after we step out. I'll also know if anyone tampers with it. We may be powerless, but we don't have to completely roll over. That's worth some pain."

The woman who had burned a world and flew from its ashes, and the man who could kill or heal through the language of physics. He didn't think they were all that powerless, even in the den of the enemy. He held on to this new feeling and stood straighter: chest big, chin up.

One of the soldiers halted at the bottom of the ramp and gestured over their shoulder with a long-barreled glave. "Out."

Sentace strode at Evi's side as they followed the soldier. The plethora of armored personnel and the generally militant aura didn't unsettle Sentace in the least, but the surroundings did. Gone was the open sky, wild air, and living things of the natural world. Scents had been scrubbed from this air. Sterile lighting cast across industrial architecture. This sector was a hive of productivity and busyness, a working organism. The spaces were either cavernous or warrenous, loud with the roar of ships and transportation, or deceptive with the quiet hum of surveillance and security.

Sentace was struck by the *variety* in the workforce, which

Trowan society had been devoid of. Some species he recognized from his tourist guests over the years, but most were new. Some had gaseous forms, some were so tiny he hardly noticed them, and others were composed of swarms difficult to parse, or in bodies only partially within his sensory range.

The facility was built around existing universe bubbles in a way that utilized the rinds as portals, spanning doorways, so only certain species or materials could cross. A genius means of control or precaution. Somewhere, there were definitely labs using universe specs for science applications, the way Sentace did with cooking.

He'd been expecting a copy of Trow, as if every large organization took the same regimented, rule-bound, hyper-vigilant shape. The energy here was chaotic and diverse.

A few passages in, at what appeared to be a sorting hub, they were dumped in the presence of a hybrid human man whose lumpy skeletal structure was jammed in untailored utilitarian clothes of Casthen black and red. Except for a crown of cranial protrusions—or perhaps horns?—his features were hard to make out past the projected holosplays surrounding him like an armor of data.

"I head Anomalous Projects," he introduced with an air of preoccupied indifference. "I understand you identified and retrieved our rogue signal. However, I'm confused." The officer finally pulled his attention away from his fifty other tasks. He leaned one direction then the next while peering at Sentace, then Evi, straight in the eyes. "Same raciation. You're Trowan like Evi Omai, which is too rare to be a coincidence, so either you stowed away on her ship and she lied—"

Sentace cut him off. What an annoying voice. "I was tracking her here and got apprehended for... contentious reasons. I became part of your last expendables drop. Check the list."

The officer did no such thing. He only had eyes for Evi, and they were full of disdain. "Well then, congratulations on succeeding my program," he said to Sentace, flat as a rock. "I knew it would produce results eventually." He flicked a couple fingers in Evi's direction and caught eyes with the soldier escorts. "Take her to extractive processing."

"What?" Evi tensed like a wild animal as soldiers grabbed her arms. "My initiation mission was separate from him! My deal is with Rennaw. Call her."

"You expect me to believe you spoke with Foremaster Rennaw?" The man's disdain curdled into outrage. "This is *my* program. You were not part of the drops, not eligible for its commendation, and this is not a negotiation."

A snarl was growing on Evi's face. If her arms hadn't been ringed in white-knuckle grips, Sentace was positive she would have punched the officer. Sentace would have helped out because this wasn't about merit at all. This was interdepartmental squabbles or about Evi's gender or just an asshole taking out a bad day on someone no one would defend. The man's best interest was probably to toss them both aside and take any credit or accolade for the find.

Voice acidic, Evi countered, "Your drop groups never would have found the anomaly. It required a ship. *My* ship."

"The Casthen's ship."

Evi's eyes went wide with the new, sharp pain of a home about to be torn away. Before she could retort, the officer nodded past her and snapped a finger. A brawny chketin lumbered over and encircled her entire upper arm in one hand while his other palm covered half her face. The group jerked Evi sideways toward another sterile hallway to elsewhere.

Sentace's feet moved before he was aware of it. He surged after her only to be blocked by the officer and a remaining solider. For a moment he did stop, as something of his old self reared up...

the version of him that would have let Evi go and seized this opportunity for self-preservation.

Sentace could see that part of himself clearly enough now to crush and discard. He and Evi had built this opportunity together. He would take one more leap of faith.

He drew himself up, taller and thicker than the officer or the soldier. He unclipped the leashes on his anger, his bloodlust, his unresolved frustration with the weeks that had transpired. If there was anywhere good to unload all that, here it was.

With threatening calm, he ordered, "Call her back."

Almost simultaneously, Evi yelled, "Rennaw!"

Sentace followed Evi's eye line to a matronly figure swishing by on the other side of the big atrium. He poured his energy in Rennaw's direction, easily pushing through the officer and the crowd. "*Foremaster!*"

Her head turned. Sentace strode with purpose, chin high, sufficiently brazen or intimidating to stop her in her tracks. He said, "Evi Omai has recovered the anomaly and is prepared for you to make good on your promise."

"Omai?" Rennaw drawled while raising a hand. A holosplay sprang to life over her slender palm, information hung on a grid of air and bent light. Minuscule finger movements scrolled her database.

Rennaw was a saisn, which explained why Evi felt she would be reasonable. Sentace had served his share of saisn ambassadors. Rennaw was taller than him, svelte, and austere, with skin storm-grey over fine musculature. The core in her forehead, an extension of the brain, was exposed among delicate bone structure and velvety skin folds. Light pooled in it as she turned. Through the saisn sense-sea, she would pick up physiological and emotional facts too subtle for human senses.

"Oh, wonderful," Rennaw said when she'd found the relevant record. She looked around for Evi but instead spotted the officer in charge. "Ah. Anomalous Projects. I should have known the noise was you."

An electric mood crackled in the air. The officer unconsciously tried to stretch his spine to match the Foremaster's height, but came up two heads too short. He cleared his throat. "This man recovered the anomaly and is part of the disposable search schedule, over which you have no oversight."

Great... separate departments had been handling the same task. How did Çydanza run such a simultaneously competent and disorganized faction? She allowed enough autonomy that corruption could grow, yet ruled with a fist iron enough to monopolize trade routes, stranglehold economies, and network across the multiverse with little opposition. Had it all grown too vast to manage, while she remained unwilling to relinquish control? Maybe if he and Evi were recruited, he would get to meet her, this being whose true form no one knew or spoke of, seemingly ageless and deathless, impossible to reach. He might see how idiocy and omnipotence could exist in one being.

Sentace forced himself to stamp down all this rage he'd summoned.

Rennaw made an unfamiliar but threatening three-finger gesture at the soldiers restraining Evi. They tensed instantly. "Stop being fools. The anomaly is my overarching jurisdiction. You've seen what that means."

Sentace had never witnessed anyone back off so swiftly as the trio surrounding Evi. Even the chketin hunched sheepishly. Sentace liked Rennaw right away. Joining the Casthen might not be so bad if he could align with the right people.

The Foremaster turned to Sentace. "I have one recruitment

- ESSA HANSEN -

position: hers. As you were part of the drop groups, you cannot fall under my arrangement, and thus are expendable once again."

"He's not," Evi vouched before the asshole officer could interject. She blocked eye line to him by rushing to Sentace's side. "The traits you saw in me, Rennaw, why you risked your position to give me this opportunity—he has those too. He showed his mettle. They dropped him out there with nothing, and he survived by using the planet's dangers to his advantage. He functions highly in any environment, no matter how unfamiliar. What better mission specialist to have? I thought the Casthen's whole business was to take up the discards of the world and make them excellent. Please, Foremaster Rennaw, look into his background."

Sentace crossed his arms and smiled at the praise.

"I did look into it," the officer butted in. "He's a cook. There's one of those on every station, Den, and civilized planet across the multiverse."

Evi cut him off: "But not *this* cook. Aren't the Casthen an organization that exploits value and prizes rarity? Rennaw, you know what the light side of this planet is like, not to mention the extra trials Anomalous Projects imposed. No mere cook could survive."

Scrutinizing Sentace, Rennaw's gaze stopped on his arms. What did all his inks and minerals and chemicals and air pockets look like through her saisn senses? Was he a new kind of monster? Most saw the surface imagery rather than the materials, and sought to extrapolate a story out of the symbolism he'd chosen, not knowing there was a code he'd picked for the shapes, elements, creatures, and geometries of his markings. A saisn might instead see him carrying around a world's worth of fragments of physical life.

The ridged musculature in Rennaw's face and neck tensed

into furrows. Intrigue.

Sentace inclined his head in the respectful way and made a gesture of joined fingertips. He summoned every nuance of saisn cultural formality he'd memorized during decades of service. "Sentace Ketch. At yours."

Rennaw hesitated in surprise, then returned the gesture before flicking through her holosplay database and stopping, ostensibly, on whatever information had been gathered about him before he was shoved on the dropship. Her midnight eyes widened. "You are indeed a culinarian. Peculiar. And you specialize in..."

She paused long enough that the officer opened his mouth to make a noise. She snapped, "Get out of my sight. A particular Enforcer is meeting me here, and did you know he does not *like* *you*?"

The officer huffed, unsure what to do with his feet or his eyes for several moments before he hustled off.

Evi pressed her shoulder against Sentace's in victory.

He drew a deep breath and picked up where Rennaw had left off. "I specialize in transuniversal effects, including crossover translation, rind qualities, and intra-universal specs."

"Endlessly applicable." Pleased, Rennaw closed her fingers, and the holosplay with it.

Sentace bowed his head again. They'd nearly won.

"Rennaw." Evi couldn't choke down the stitch of nervousness in her voice. "Is there a place here for both of us?"

"You pass muster for myself, but I am in no position to make promises. You will both undergo the customary inspection, interview, and initiation around whatever criteria a candidate department requires. We would assess your merit, value, and ideal placement, then discuss what gear, tools, ship upgrades, and other resources you would be requiring."

A sparkly feeling danced through Sentace. Support. Tools. *Re-sources*. The Trowan government would never.

Evi slid a palm between his shoulder blades. As good as a hug. "The opportunity is more than enough for now," she said. "Thank you. Glad to see not all Casthen are..." She caught herself and trailed off.

Rennaw finished, "Assholes and shit-stirrers, yes. The reason I first saw merit in you, Omai, is because you are not one of them, but you will stand your ground against them. We need more of that here if anything of value is to get done. Now—follow me lest another one spots us."

Before Evi drifted away, Sentace wrapped both arms around her shoulders and pulled her in for a proper hug. He pressed his cheek against her hair and whispered, "Through the first part of the labyrinth."

"Mm." She squeezed him back for a second then shoved. "Let go. You still smell like that damned ocean."

15

NOPHEK

"I'll try it first." Sentace sounded confident but didn't feel it yet.

"Wha' if after, you 'ave *no skin*?" Chiidi wailed.

Evi clicked her tongue. "Then he'd still be cleaner."

Sentace, Evi, and Chiidi stood before the newly installed scour beside the engine room door on the lower level of Evi's ship. It was by far the most expensive of the upgrades the Casthen had provided as recruitment bonuses—pricier than Sentace's portable kitchen station—but the technicians hadn't tested it post-installation. Sentace was realizing that operating within the Casthen was this unnatural balance of being tightly overseen at times, but needing to look out entirely for oneself at others.

Evi slapped him on the back. "In with you."

"You prefer skinless men, huh."

"*In.*"

The scour was a cylindrical space designed to accommodate most species. The walls were translucent but dotted with internal bubbles. Sweet chemical fragrances lingered alongside the grease scent of the mechanics' work.

Fully clothed in loose trousers and a tight jacket, Sentace stepped into the scour. The door slid shut and sealed. The luminous lavender-colored walls faded to midnight blue, his cue to hold his breath.

The process was a symphony of sensations he had trouble parsing in the handful of heartbeats it took to happen. A hiss dropped to a bass rumble. Light swirled across his eyelids in colors too quick to catch. Heat flushed from his core outward, then a cold snap, on to dense waves of vibration tumbling over him like a deep tissue massage. He grew warm, lightweight, energized, his bowels emptied, skin and hair cleaned, small cuts and abrasions and bruises healed... Sentace promised himself he would never take this device for granted.

The door rotated open to Evi, suppressing a smile. "And there he is, skin and all."

"Chiidi's turn!" The iredimi squeezed between Sentace's legs and bundled themself inside before he'd finished exiting. Their fur had dried into a dingy, clumpy situation after the river soak.

Evi snorted a laugh. Sentace stood next to her, feeling soft and refreshed. He ran a hand through his now silky hair, which he'd cut short a while ago.

The scour process was calmer from the outside. It opened to reveal Chiidi so fluffy their features were almost entirely obscured. Their mouth opened huge and froggy, their parabola ears twitched in excitement, and their inky eyes glistened. Their fur was as white as fresh snow, with a downy undercoat that had a nacreous sheen.

"So *dry!*" Chiidi raced up to the cargo bay while clicking with laughter.

Sentace said, "We might have to put a daily limit on scour use."

Evi hummed. "Once each day for you two, and however much I want."

"Jito now!" Chiidi called from above.

"Don't even try it." Sentace headed up to police them while Evi tucked herself into the scour. She shed her morphcoat and threw it at his back before the door closed. Its delicate technology couldn't be scoured—a shame because it still smelled and looked stained from contact with the anomaly. A Graven stain? He would consider it a souvenir of their accomplishment.

Part of Sentace's most recent exhaustion was from the logistical gymnastics required to keep Chiidi and Jito from being discovered during multiple phases of Casthen inspections, interviews, and hazing. Chiidi had hated being smuggled back and forth between cargo and sleeping quarters and baggage, and was a firecracker of pent-up energy now that they'd gotten off-planet.

Sentace's life continued to be a rhythm of wildly good and bad luck: he and Evi had been allowed to skip the formal Casthen initiation—a psychological interrogation by the Casthen's leader, Çydanza—in order to take on another unique mission similar to tracking the anomaly. Being only half-Casthen or whatever, they had been kept unconscious during the trip away from headquarters so they'd remain ignorant of where that planet was located or how it was accessed.

In a way, Sentace was homeless and cut adrift again, but he found it a comfortable exchange for the opportunity to stay paired up with Evi and their two stowaways.

Chiidi had already showed themself to have a knack for languages and cultural negotiation. They were a little social chameleon and a natural at cons, plus small enough to sneak around.

Jito had been rebottled in a container more like its former

brainpan, with a fluid culture suitable for scholm. They couldn't yet afford access to the equipment or synthetic body parts that would allow it to communicate. Evi now entertained notions of Jito becoming an ally and being their crew's muscle in a new mechanical body. Sentace hoped it held a position of power in some syndicate or another, so they could extort it for resources in exchange for its freedom. In the meantime, the creature's jar had a place in the bay where it could observe everything while they continued to inadvertently form a fictional personality around it.

Evi ascended, freshly scoured. She let her long, wavy hair down and scrubbed her fingernails through her scalp. A pleased, feline look crimped her lips.

Sentace threw her morphcoat back at her. It transformed from scales into a gauzy knit.

He joined her in the cockpit alcove, which sparkled with an upgraded holosplay. A map expanded to capacity, showing the massive foam of bubble universes comprising their current galactic structure. Beyond that and the cockpit windows lay a view of stars, nebulae, galaxies... the view that over decades had fired Evi's soul toward revolution. Sentace, lacking such a view all his younger life, was new to this invigorating feeling of immense *smallness*.

Chiidi joined them but skirted around the stain the anomaly had made on the ship's floor.

Sentace waved to zoom the map out even more. The chartings they had been allowed to download from the Casthen were limited. "Where to start?"

"Well. We need you to pore over all this and select some candidate universes. Then I'll find the most efficient egress chains to route us there, and you verify that the crossovers are safe."

"That's a lot of the most boring work I can think of."

"That's where to start." Evi shot him a sympathetic look. "But we have no solid time frame and our intel is limited, so let's do something fun? The Cartographers have more charting, but we'd need funds or have to explore uncharted space to exchange for them. How about we head to the uncharted edges of the multiverse first and find ways to gain currency along the route? We can't go completely rogue without the Casthen's tracker making them yank our leash, but there are plenty of places to explore within allowance."

The tension sluiced from Sentace's body. "Better."

Evi petted the top of Chiidi's head and glanced back at Jito. "These two limit the crossovers we can take on and the universes we can enter. Are you sure you're up to calculating compatibility every single time we go somewhere new?"

"I'm done living in a group that's all the same. No one grows that way."

Evi's smile felt like sunshine. "Agreed. Alright. Let's start hunting down another impossible thing together."

Sentace didn't quite understand the mission the Casthen had given them, but it came with the freedom he'd hoped for. Their task had a complexion that he couldn't explain except that it felt like ending up in that dropship, then meeting Evi, then finding the anomaly after all. Inevitability. Synchronicity. Design. Deeply ominous.

Invigorating.

Sentace and Evi had been tasked with finding—if one existed in the entirety of the multiverse—a universe with intensely specific parameters, which encapsulated a habitable planet with a very specific environment. They hadn't been told what the Casthen were plotting to use it for. As with the anomaly, finding it might allow the Casthen to accomplish immense harm, or incredible good. Or both.

Sentace was a prime candidate for the mission for obvious reasons, and Evi had aced the pilot trials even with her work-in-progress ship. They had made a strong case to go together since this did feel so similar to the challenge of the anomaly.

Their objective would be obscenely rare, if it even existed.

The mission could take years. Perhaps their lifetime.

Might as well have fun being free in the meantime.

Evi draped herself in the pilot's seat and donned her neural halo, which settled nicely around a new implant. "I'm hungry. Where first, chef?"

Sentace poked around the map at the hazy edges of the multiverse and found a strand of habitable planets barely explored, marked high priority by the Cartographers. A tourist hub sat nearby. "Here. I can build up my name and customer base. Ah—we still need to fake your death and send proof to Trow so they can make a big deal about it."

"Can I pick how I die?"

"As long as it's plausible. Knives, poisons, shoved into the wrong world—"

"Knives. We'll get you a nice big one at the next stop."

ACKNOWLEDGMENTS

This story wouldn't have happened without Richard Swan throwing my name in the hat, Beth Tabler being a long-time supporter, and Adrian Collins giving me a chance. Adrian's honesty, transparency, communication, and inclusion has been a breath of fresh air in an industry where profit often comes before kindness.

As ever, I owe dearly to the beta readers who helped me hammer out the story's flaws and protect its effective parts. They are all fantastic authors—please check out their books: Sunyi Dean (*The Book Eaters*), Wayne Santos (*The Chimera Code*), Ryan Rose (*Seven Recipes for Revolution*), Gautam Bhatia (*The Sentence*), Al Hess (*World Running Down*), Darby Harn (*Ever The Hero*), and Rachel Fikes (*Keeper of Sorrows*).

I was thrilled to have Ed Crocker's absolutely spot-on edits (including knowledge of the trilogy!). Thank you for the laughs and for enduring all the commas I still can't get right.

Cheers to Carlos Diaz for tackling a difficult concept with the bubble multiverse on the novella's cover. Much love to Pen Astridge for finding trilogy-matching typography, designing the interior, and for creating such beautiful promotional materials.

To all the readers who finished *The Graven trilogy* and said they've wanted to revisit that world or stay a little longer...Your enthusiasm makes it possible to write spinoff snacks like this novella. Keep being vocal about the books you love.